Books

by

Sara V. Zook

The 'Strange in Skin' Trilogy

Strange in Skin # 1

Evadere # 2

Solace # 3

Stand-alone novel

Clipped

Co-authored with Wendy S. Chartier

The 'Sempiternal Series'

Evanescent #1

Evadere

Sara V. Zook

Planettopia Publishing

Evadere

Planettopia Publishing

Copyright © 2012 by Sara V. Zook

ISBN-10: 194124694X

ISBN-13: 978-1-941246-94-8

This book is dedicated to my beautiful niece, Riley Grace Payne, who has been a blessing to my life since the day she was born.

Prologue

Atavia sat straight up in bed, beads of sweat already forming at her temples. Her heart raced as she tried to remain perfectly still, listening. There it was again, another blood curdling, shrill scream. It belonged to the servant, Jillianne.

She leapt from the bed, her head dizzy in panic. Where was the baby? Jillianne shrieked again. The noise sounded closer this time, echoing off the walls of the stone hallway. Then she heard a noise that almost made her heart stop altogether. The baby cried at the top of his lungs as if he were in pain. She sprinted out of the room and ran directly into Jillianne.

"Oh, Atavia! Atavia!" Jillianne cried out, wrapping herself around the woman's leg as she babbled in fear.

Atavia tried to kick her off her leg.

"Get up!" she commanded, her voice quivering now as she did so. "What's wrong? Get hold of yourself."

Jillianne slowly climbed to her feet as she stared upward at her Queen. "It's just so terrible! I'm so sorry this has happened!" Tears streamed down her face.

"What is it?" She grabbed Jillianne by the shoulders and tried to steady her. "What did you see?"

"The Scaves ..."

Atavia covered her mouth in horror. "Here? Now?" Jillianne nodded as she lowered her head.

"But how? How'd they get past the guards?"

Atavia fled to the veranda where her hands gripped the railing tight. Her guards lie in pools of blood on the castle floor, spears piercing through their torsos, their lifeless eyes looking straight up at their magnificent Queen. She felt as if the breath had been sucked out of her lungs. The baby. Where was her baby?

She grabbed both sides of her long, flowing nightgown and sprinted down the hallway to her precious little boy. Tears began to sting her own eyes as the image of blood covering the once very strong guards that they had called friends now haunted her. She almost screamed when she entered the room.

"Give him to me!" a Scave demanded, a sword with a glistening, sharp point aimed directly at her husband's throat as he grasped tightly onto the frightened baby and held him behind his back for protection.

"You're as good as dead, I hope you know," Calan threatened the savage man, hatred filling his eyes that his home had been attacked in the middle of the night. He looked up then and saw her standing in the doorway. Their eyes locked on one another. This couldn't be the end. They had worked too hard to let this be it. Calan gave her a little nod. She read his mind.

An eerie growl escaped the intruder's mouth as he now pressed the blade against the skin of Calan's neck.

With one swift motion, the king tossed the baby through the air at Atavia. She scrambled toward him and caught the baby, pressing his quivering body against her own warm chest.

The Scave roared in fury. Atavia's eyes grew large in panic as Calan desperately swatted the sword away from his throat and leapt in the air toward the intruder. The Ashen swung the blade around again, the tip of it piercing through the King's throat. Blood gushed upward, covering the dirt- stained skin of the savage.

Atavia's knees buckled. She was about to collapse, but the baby let out another cry. She huddled him even tighter. The Scave turned to stare at her. Calan's blood dripped down his hairy face, exposing sharp teeth.

Atavia turned and ran. She didn't notice the chill of the stone steps against her bare feet, nor the oozing, still warm blood as she stomped through the pools as she's going past the dead guards, dots of crimson speckling her white nightgown. She didn't bother looking back to see if the fierce Scave was following her. She couldn't. She had to keep going.

The blackness of the night filled Atavia's vision as she hurried toward the soft grasses that soon towered over her head as she continued running, her mind focused on escape. She felt someone wrap their arms around her waist. As she fell to the ground with the baby tucked underneath her, she spun hard and landed on her back, the baby safe in her arms.

"Shhh!" someone hissed.

Atavia's eyes searched the darkness for a face.

"It's me. Ben."

Her heart fluttered with hope for a moment. "Did I outrun him?"

The baby squirmed in her arms. She prayed he wouldn't let out a loud cry.

Ben remained quiet for a moment before turning toward her again. "Yes, I think he expected you to go toward the village, but we have to be careful. There has to be others waiting."

She shuddered at the strength the Scaves had had to kill all of her guards and her strong King.

"He's gone," Jillianne hissed, now hurrying over to Atavia, crouching low in the grasses herself. "You ran away?" Atavia asked her. Jillianne sighed in shame.

"Coward." Atavia's temper flared.

"She couldn't have saved you," Ben said.

Atavia ran her fingertips along the soft skin of the baby's head. It had taken so long for them to have this child, and how her heart ached now knowing that the savages wanted him dead so badly that they would resort to something like this.

"Calan's dead." She tried to blink away the gruesome scene in her head. "They're not going to stop until they get what they want."

Ben touched the chest of the baby. "You have to let him go, Atavia."

The tears streamed down her face. She didn't want to hear those words, but she knew that Ben simply spoke the truth. "It's so hard. I don't know if I can."

Jillianne made her way over beside the sobbing Queen and put an arm around her shoulder. "You know what you have to do."

"It's such an awful place, though. Those humans are ..."

"Savages?" Ben asked.

Atavia knew he was right. Human evil couldn't be worse than what was going on here. The Scaves would murder him for sure if he stayed here in the world he belonged to, in the world he should be reigning over. "You've already made arrangements, haven't you, Ben?"

"Yes."

Atavia heard screaming in the distance. Were the Scaves going to kill everyone in their search for the baby prince? She pressed her face down into the neck of the baby, breathing in his scent and felt her tears against his warm skin. "I love you, always." And with that, she handed the only child she would ever have over to Ben, who gave only one moment's hesitation before hurrying away. Atavia gripped onto Jillianne and broke into violent sobs.

Chapter 1

"She's dead."

I looked up at Emry. It was the third time he had said those words in the past five minutes. We sat side by side, my hand resting on his knee. His eyes were glued on the coffin.

People were beginning to come in now and fill the seats of the funeral home. I glanced back once and met the curious eyes of some older ladies seated behind us.

"I don't know why these people are even bothering," he whispered, his head lowered as he stared at the floor.

"Come on, Emry," I said. "It's her funeral."

He shook his head in disagreement and ran a hand quickly through his hair. "They aren't coming for her." His eyes glanced up at the coffin, and then returned to the floor. "They're here for the show."

"What show?"

"Don't you see what they're all staring at?"

I turned my head toward the back of the room. I felt everyone's eyes shift to my face. I leaned even further into Emry's side. "They're staring at me."

He nodded. "You, me, us. They're here to see us together."

The preacher came down the aisle and stopped at Emry's side. He hunched over to whisper in Emry's ear. "Would you like to say a few words?"

Emry shifted in his seat and hesitated for a moment. "No. I just ... don't have anything to say."

The preacher glanced my way for a moment before continuing up to the front of the room toward the corpse.

I felt a sudden cool breeze touch my calf. Emry and I both turned to look toward the doors located at the back of the room. A group of men, six in total, entered. They were all tall, lean, and dressed in expensive black suits. Their eyes were dark and piercing as they stared directly at Emry.

"Who are they?" I whispered.

He reached over and grabbed my hand tightly. "I don't know. I don't have a good feeling about this."

Me either. My stomach churned as the tension in the small room grew by the moment. I closed my eyes and attempted to breathe normally. What was going on here?

"Please, take your seats everyone, so we can begin the service," the preacher said in front of us as he took his place behind the small pulpit.

Emry kept glancing at the strange group of men. They didn't sit down, but continued to stand in a semi-circle in the back of the room near the wall. His hand trembled as I held onto it. "Emry, are you okay?"

He stood, his eyes locked on the men in the back. He took a step backward. They took a step toward us.

Emry yanked me to my feet. The churning in my stomach increased to nausea. I felt as if I would vomit.

"Mr. Logan?" the preacher's voice rang out from behind us in a questioning tone. He, too, was clueless as to what was happening.

The uneasiness increased as if we were all poised for battle, like we were the prey and any sudden movements would get us killed. Who were these men? Why were they in the funeral home? I could tell they were after Emry as they barricaded us in, the room now becoming another coffin, one large enough for the both of us.

"We have to leave," Emry stated. "Now."

He gripped the back of my arm and moved another step backward. The men moved a step closer again, angry scowls on their faces. Their eyes gleamed with a fierce hatred.

With one swift movement, Emry turned and rushed toward the emergency exit, my arm almost popping out of its socket as he dragged me along with him. The group of men dove at us in a failed attempt to try to stop us from leaving. Then my eyes lingered on one thing before Emry had me completely out of the door, our coffin.

Rest in peace, Lainey Tritt, I thought.

The sun warmed my face as cool water brushed across my toes. I opened my eyes. What a heavenly way to awaken. I smiled. I was in heaven. I was in Evadere.

I sat up and wrapped my arms around my knees as my eyes scanned over the peaceful water. A gentle breeze rippled through, making tiny waves. I dug my toes into the silky sands and inhaled deeply.

Earlier in the day we were back on Earth at Lainey Tritt's funeral. We barely made it past the exit door before those creepy men closed in on us, and then poof, here we were, hand in hand, Emry and I, back in this wondrous place. We had been trying to sort through what had happened with those men, who they were and why they were after us, but after many failed attempts at trying to understand, we had simply given up and succumbed to the exhaustion that overcame our bodies. I had fallen asleep in Emry's strong arms, my head on his chest. My smile widened.

I glanced around. Where was Emry? He probably had taken a stroll and let me sleep. Maybe he had climbed up on the cliffs. I shaded my eyes from the sunlight as I looked up at the cliffs overhead. Nothing.

Jumping to my feet, I brushed off the white sand that stuck to the back of my legs. I hurried to the other side of the beach, my mind having frantic thoughts of being all alone in this beautiful place since Emry wasn't anywhere to be seen.

"Emry!" I cried out, with no response. "Emry!" Still no response. I desperately ran to yet another side of the beach and peered up at the majestic cliffs that towered above. I could see the whole way to the top, but he wasn't there.

I took a deep breath and tried to remain calm. I hadn't been farther than this before. The tips of the alluring golden grasses swayed rhythmically with the breeze. They were almost as high as my waist. There was an eerie attraction about them. I wanted to reach out my hand and touch them, run through them, but fear stopped me from doing so. It was almost as if I could sense the hidden evil lurking within those glorious plants. Something told me that if I were to go in there, I may not come back out.

I looked up toward the ruddy sky. It was growing darker by the moment. Surely it had to be evening.

I felt slightly dizzy and sat down in the sand looking out over the water. My stomach growled. I ignored it. A sickening feeling followed the pangs of hunger as the realization settled in of what was happening.

Emry wasn't here. I was all alone in Evadere. When I was with him, this place seemed surreal, magical and there was nowhere else I'd rather be. But without him, it all seemed too good to be true. There was something else about this place. It was as if the beauty of it all was merely a masquerade that hid something ugly waiting just below the surface.

I closed my eyes. The reality of my abandonment was haunting. He would come back for me, I was sure of it.

My eyes snapped open. I had fallen asleep in the sand. It was nighttime now. I couldn't help but stare into the sky, the whitish stars so large, so bright as if I could reach out and touch them. Then the reality that I was still in Evadere without Emry hit me. My hungry belly protested against its emptiness. I took a deep breath and tried to will the slight ache away.

A scraping sound in the distance alarmed me. My eyes darted around, searching in the darkness for an answer of where it had come from. I waited, remaining absolutely still.

It came again, only this time even closer. It sounded as if someone were walking, their steps heavy as if wounded, like one of their feet dragged behind them. Anxiety filled every ounce of my body. I kept squatted down on the balls of my feet, the tips of my fingers balancing my weight in the sand. I was ready to run if need be.

Please, please go away.

I tried to slow my now out of control breathing that came in huffs that were louder than I wanted.

What could it possibly be? I looked around in the dark. The possibilities were endless. This wasn't Earth. I had no idea of what kind of things could be lurking here on Evadere, what kind of monsters came out in the darkness.

Why did Emry leave me here? Tears stung my eyes and spilled over onto my cheeks. What was I going to do? What could I do?

I glanced toward the high golden grasses that now looked like black spikes in the dark of night.

They beckoned me in with their height; the only place where I could hide from whatever it was that was coming.

My pulse raced as the noise came again. It sounded close, as if it were right next to me this time.

My fingers ached from the position I had them in, forcing them to bear most of my weight. I didn't dare move a muscle.

My eyes searched the darkness from where I thought the noise had been coming from. The only sound was my labored breaths.

I caught sight of a shadow standing a few feet away on my left. I could only make out a small form.

Never before had I felt such a fierce terror rip through my entire body. The adrenaline coursed through my veins at full speed, and my head throbbed as I tried to remain perfectly still. Neither one of us moved as we stared at each other's shadowy forms under the glorious stars on a beach too beautiful not to be cursed with something demonic.

Then it reached out its limbs toward me as it took a heavy step forward. It only took half a second to register that if I didn't move right now,

I would be the meal of this unknown creature standing so close it could possibly slaughter me in one swift movement. Without hesitation, I launched my body away from it and took off as fast as I could toward the golden grasses in the distance. I didn't stop and didn't look back until I felt the plants suck me into their grasp. I ran farther into them until my lungs

burned in agony and I couldn't take another step. I collapsed to the ground, the plants hovering above my head. I panted wildly, trying to suck more oxygen into my lungs. I put my hand over my chest and could feel my heart thumping madly within my skin.

Oh, please, God, let me have escaped.

I closed my eyes and tried to shut out the torments that I had just forced upon my body. The adrenaline slowly began to recede.

Something warm touched my arm. An ear-piercing, shrill scream escaped from my throat. "Are you okay?" someone whispered.

I lapped air into my lungs. My muscles were on fire from the strain. I struggled to see clearly in the dark, even with those stars seeming so bright, so near.

"Who is it?" I hissed. "Who's there?"

"Jo."

I composed myself as quickly as possible and jumped to my feet. Beside me stood a little girl, the top of her head only reaching to my shoulder. I couldn't see her entirely.

"We have to get out of here," I whispered to her quickly. "There's something after me." The girl just stood there in silence.

"Did you hear what I said? We have to leave."

"What's after you?" she finally asked.

She was wasting time. That thing could be here at any moment, although I didn't hear it coming like

I had before. "I don't know. It was back there beside me on the beach."

"You think I'm after you?"

"What? No," I answered, now getting irritated with how calm and still she was being. Couldn't she sense my urgency? "It was back there in the sand. It was standing right next to me. I don't know what it was."

"I was standing next to you over there," she confessed.

"What?" My head spun from trying to process it all. "It couldn't have been you. It was making a noise, like it was dragging something or part of itself. I don't know."

She reached out and touched my arm. "That was me. I was dragging a heavy sack behind me. I left it back there. I thought you were hurt."

"Oh," I managed to get out.

"Are you still frightened by me?" she asked.

Now I just felt irritated that I had ran away from a child. "Well, no, not now that I know what you are."

"You know what I am?" She sounded alarmed now.

I couldn't say she was a human, because the truth of the matter was I didn't know what she was if she came from this place. "Jo, was it?"

She hesitated.

I wondered why this little girl was out here by herself in the middle of the night. "Thanks for checking on me," I added, trying not to scare her off. Right now, I didn't want to be alone. I welcomed her company with open arms.

"Yeah, Jo."

"I'm Anna," I introduced myself. "I'm … lost."

"Lost?" Jo sounded confused by the statement. "Why are you alone? Are you running from someone?"

"I was with someone," I told her. "But I don't know where he is now." Jo's silence was beginning to disturb me. She was a nervous, little creature, yet she was out here all alone in the dark.

"Are you sick? You don't seem quite right."

"I was scared …"

"No," she interrupted. "That's not it."

We stood there for a few moments in the dark. I felt as if she could see me way better than I could her.

"What is your contribution?" Jo finally asked, her voice seeming to become more afraid of me by the minute.

"I'm sorry. I don't know what you're talking about," I confessed. Here we were, two strangers in the dark, trying to figure one another out. For all I knew, she could have fangs and green skin, but from what I could tell, she seemed so much like a child.

"Where are you from?" she asked.

I hesitated. I might as well tell her. Maybe she would know how to get out of here. "Earth." Jo took a step backward, tripped, and fell on her back. I hesitantly extended my hand to her.

Feeling what felt like a normal hand and fingers, I helped her up. Pulling her back to her feet seemed effortless as there wasn't much weight on her small frame. Once standing, she still continued to move backward.

"What is it? Did I say something wrong?" I whispered. I had obviously alarmed her.

"You're human?"

"Yes," I said slowly. "You know what that is?"

Jo inched away even more.

"Please!" I cried out. "Don't go. I don't know how to get back. Please, I'm hungry. Can you at least tell me how to get food?" I felt myself move forward, closer to her.

The girl stopped. "I can't help you."

"Why not?" I asked.

"You're a human."

Human. I wondered what the word meant to her, but she obviously wasn't going to stick around long enough for me to question her further about the subject. "Look, Jo." I forced a smile in case she really could see me. "I just need a little help getting food. Then I won't bother you again.

I'm going to just get something to eat and then go right back over ..." I turned my head to the left toward the beach. It was gone. I turned my entire body around as my eyes frantically searched for the water. Then I looked down in horror. I was no longer standing in the golden grasses. They, too, were nowhere to be seen. I was standing on solid, barren ground. I lifted my foot and put it back down again. I could hear the noise of the dry ground crumbling beneath my shoe. "Where did it go?"

"The sand and water?" she asked.

"Yes." My eyes kept scanning the area behind me over and over again, hoping with all my might that it would return. "How do I get back to it?"

Jo exhaled loudly. "You can't."

"What?" The word stuck in my throat. "This doesn't make sense. It was just right there ..."My voice trailed off. I stared out into the nothingness. It felt like I was in some sort of nightmare and would never wake up. I closed my eyes tight. Emry had to have transported by himself unknowingly, but he would be trying, I knew, to figure out how to get back to me on the beach. "Please." My voice began to shake along with my entire body. "I know nothing about this place. I'm begging you."

Jo was silent for a long while, but she didn't back away any farther.

"Can you just point me in the right direction?"

"I don't know what you want," she finally said.

I wanted Emry to be here. He'd know what to do. He could take us both back to Earth. I decided I should just start small with this girl. She was obviously skittish near me, now that she knew I was human. I just needed to gain a little trust from her. Who knew if the next someone I met would be as nice as she was, or even if there would be another someone.

I licked my dry lips. "Food. Anything. Something. Please."

"Ok," she whispered.

A small amount of relief washed over me. "Yeah?" I asked, still afraid to get too close to her in case she'd take off running.

"I walk fast," she warned me.

I nodded. "I'll keep up."

"Stay close."

I took another look behind me at what used to be a beautiful, familiar place where Emry had first exposed his secret to me, where we had first kissed and promised each other we'd figure it all out together in our new sense of freedom. A kind of nothingness stared right back at me as a pulsing ache began to grow in my temples. How would Emry ever be able to find me now?

Chapter 2

Jo was a very fast walker, but I kept up even though I felt like I was mostly jogging.

As morning changed the darkness into a pale light, I was relieved to see that she was just a normal little girl. Skinny and short with long brown, straight hair that reached her waist and fluttered in the wind as she moved. Her clothes were much worn, appearing to have been cut or ripped at the sleeves and waist. She looked too fragile to be out here on her own.

We didn't speak for what seemed like hours, just walked on. Exhaustion settled into the depths of my out of shape physique.

Everything was barren. No signs of plants or life anywhere. A ground composed of grayish-colored dust crunched beneath my feet with every step. The horizon was full of more lifeless colors, everything except the sky, which still remained a pale red with bright, enormous stars.

I didn't know how I felt. Mostly, numbness consumed me. This was not how I expected Evadere to be, nor did I anticipate to explore it like this. I thought Emry and I would be walking for miles through endless golden grasses until we reached another beach even more illuminating than the last. I thought this planet was going to be rich with colors, possibly some my eyes had never seen before; a place of wondrous magic and mystery. The realization was setting in that Evadere was not a place of escape. It was one of disappointment and loneliness. I had strayed from the one place Emry could find me, and now even that had disappeared. My mind whirled with possible scenarios of what the future would hold for me here, most of them not pleasant thoughts. I didn't know what I was supposed to do, how anyone survived here, let alone by myself, and I couldn't figure out a way to get back to Emry. I had no powers. Tears stung my eyes, but I quickly wiped them away with the back of my hand and continued on. Tears would change nothing, and I didn't want to scare away Jo. This girl was my only hope at the moment. We hadn't seen anyone else since walking most of the night and morning. A thick fog began to hover a few feet above the ground. I missed Earth. I allowed my head to slump down, my eyes cast down to my feet.

"There."

I jerked my head up. She pointed to a place so far ahead of us, I could barely see it in the distance. "What is that?" I asked, my throat burning from the dust that had been kicked up along the way.

"Where we can get food," she said, almost in a whisper.

All I could make out was a green dot. "There are others there?"

She nodded, her dark eyes large in anticipation.

"Are they friendly?" I squeezed my right hand into a tight ball.

"Not to us."

Before I could ask anything more, Jo was back to walking fast again.

At the first sight of trees, I felt a warm exhilaration zip through my veins, but at the same time, the sight was eerie. The ground just went from dusty, lifeless trails drained of color to bright greens and dark browns as plants swayed in the gentle breeze ahead and the dirt looked so fresh and full of nutrients it was as if someone painted this glorious scene on a canvas. It was like a hologram. As soon as my bare feet touched the soft, lush grass, a tingle danced its way upon my skin. Evadere was back to being breathtaking once again.

"Lower yourself," Jo commanded.

I instantly crouched down behind a gigantic tree that was almost as round as it was tall. I peered around the side of it, wanting to see more of what this place beheld.

Jo grabbed my arm sternly. "Careful," she warned.

I raised my eyebrows in concern. "What is this place?"

She wrapped her arms around her knees in a child-like manner and rocked on the balls of her feet.

"These are the farming contributors."

"Contributors." I let the word roll off of my tongue for a moment. "That's the second time you've said that. What does it mean exactly?"

She peered at me, giving me a look as if judging my intelligence. "This group of contributors grows vegetables and fruits for the planet to eat."

The ground looked very fertile and good for growing crops. "How does this happen?"

"What?"

"The ground just went from dust to grass. Where is the boundary?" I questioned her.

"Where the contributors' powers end."

My mind was spinning. I was hungry, tired, worried, and now trying to figure out how a whole new planet existed and continued to exist. I felt a little dizzy and then made a quick attempt to shake it off. "They contribute food ..." I began.

"Uh huh," Jo replied.

"For everyone else?"

She nodded. "For all other contributors. Not Scaves."

"Scaves?"

"Contributors hate Scaves."

Jo climbed back into a standing position. She pressed one hand against the tree bark and carefully peeked out and around the massive plant.

"What are you doing?" I asked.

She put a finger up to her lips to silence me. Then, without taking her eyes off of whatever it was she was looking at, she motioned for me to come over to her.

"Jo?" I whispered.

"We have to make our move. Now."

I felt my eyebrows move upward, but couldn't find the courage to speak. She was being so cautious with her movements, and I wanted so desperately to know what she was looking at … or for.

"Ready?" she hissed.

"What ..." Before I could finish, I watched frail, little Jo dart off and away from the protection of the tree. Rushing to her side, I found myself in the middle of a field with endless rows of crops. Every plant extended upward from the luscious dirt as they flourished perfectly from the ground beneath them. I touched a leaf as I allowed the velvety warmth to caress my fingertips. The smell of ripened fruits filled the air with a sweet aroma. I inhaled deeply and pressed my face toward the sun.

Sudden movement caught my eye as one of the plants in the corner of the field shook. I could make out the form of a person bent over toward the ground.

"Quick!" Jo hissed, grabbing my hand and pulling me with her. We rushed over to the nearest hiding spot by a broad gray building. Jo dove onto the ground behind it, still gripping my hand.

My feet stumbled over themselves, tumbling me face first onto the ground beside her. "Ouch," I cried out.

"Shhh!" Jo shot me a disapproving glare.

I winced from the sudden pain in my face where my skin had scraped against the tiny, jagged rocks surrounding the building. I touched my cheek and stared at the return of blood on my fingertips.

Climbing to my feet, I crouched down beside Jo. She was peeking out from the side of the building toward the person we had seen that had startled her. I propped myself up to be slightly taller than her so I could see, too.

This particular part of Evadere was very quiet. I wondered where all the rest of the people were.

There stood a single person, a middle-aged male, inspecting the plants of the field and collecting the ripened fruit and placing them into a sack that was positioned on the ground nearby. I watched curiously as one of the plants was hunched over, its leaves wilted as if in need of water. The man made his way over to it. He touched the base of the plant with his hand, and I gasped as the once wounded plant quickly turned to a deep shade of green like the others around it, the leaves uncurled and became full and it stood straight up toward the sun as if completely revived.

"How did ...?" I looked questioningly toward Jo.

"He's a contributor," she replied in a low whisper.

She continued to use this term. Still not fully able to comprehend what had just happened, I leaned against the wall of the building. I wrapped my arms around my knees.

"Jo," I said a little louder.

She immediately covered my mouth with her hand. I jerked back in disgust as I could taste the dirt from her palm in my mouth.

"You need to be silent," she growled, her anger increasing.

I lowered my eyebrows. "Why don't we just go over to him and tell him we're hungry? Maybe he'll just give us some food."

Jo's eyes widened in alarm. "Are you insane?"

"No," I quickly replied. "It's just ... he looks harmless and all."

Jo positioned herself so that we were face to face. She got close to me so that our noses were almost touching and I could smell her foul breath in my nostrils. She extended her arm out and pointed toward the man in the field. "That harmless contributor out there will kill you and me without hesitation." She continued to look me straight in the eye to confirm my understanding.

She was genuinely terrified of being here. "Understand, *human*?"

I gritted my teeth at the way she said human. It was obviously meant to demean me and the way I had perceived the situation at hand. "Yeah," I managed to say.

"I need you to listen to everything I tell you to do and just do it, so we can get food and make it out of here alive." She pulled herself away from my face.

I wiped tiny droplets of sweat from my forehead with the back of my hand and allowed my head to lean against the wall. "I just don't understand, Jo."

"You humans really are dense, aren't you?"

I narrowed my eyes at the once seemingly sweet and kind girl who now seemed to have this real edge to her, a bite.

"You can't have everything you want right this minute," she continued. "We don't have time to sit here and sort things through. We go on instinct. We survive."

With those jagged words still stabbing my ego, I pressed my lips tightly together and rose to my feet, making a solemn attempt to forget the dull ache on my cheek. Eyeing me still, Jo stood and then slowly went back over to the edge of the wall and looked past it. We stayed there for a few moments, me behind her staring out into the distance, into the nothingness that we had just come from in order to get here. I thought about Emry just then. I wondered where he was and how crazy he must be going not being able to find me, knowing that I was still here. This world was odd and so unfamiliar, yet I knew I had to be persistent and try to understand it all. I had to figure out a way to get back to Emry. Then a haunting thought came to mind. Perhaps he was back on Evadere and in search for me in this awful place all alone. At least I had Jo. He would have no one.

"The contributor has left. Now," Jo commanded, rushing from the safety of the building and out into the openness of the field.

I followed as fast as I could, struggling to keep up with her quickness. The field was desolate. Not a soul in sight. The limbs of the lush plants whipped my bare arms and legs as I hurried through them toward Jo, who was just a few feet ahead as she neared a section that was yet to be picked and still had fruit hanging from it.

"Do this," Jo whispered, her eyes wide in urgency.

I watched her flip the bottom of her shirt inside out as she tore fruit from its stem and tossed it into the sack she had created. She plucked off a few more before pulling the bottom up tighter and trapping the food inside her shirt. She looked up and gave me another hard stare.

Realizing I was standing there being a dense human again, I quickly tried to recover by copying her. As I grasped the first fruit into my palm, I couldn't help but notice its perfection. It was round and red, not a single mark or bruise on its skin. The story of Adam and Eve entered my mind as I held it, still connected to the stem, perplexed by the fruit's beauty and marveled in it being forbidden. My stomach twisted in hunger as I imaged its delicious juice on my tongue, yet it seemed as though once I had plucked it from the plant, things would change somehow. Emotionally overwhelmed at the sudden feeling of guilt that now filled every ounce of me, I looked back up at Jo who had jumped over into another row of plants and was collecting a smaller kind of fruit, tucking them away in her shirt that now bulged in front of her. Shaking off the weird sensation that the appearance of the fruit had given me, I thoughtlessly jerked it from its stem and placed it in my shirt. I bent down to retrieve more fruit from the bottom near the ground when I heard a shrill scream.

"Anna!"

I searched for Jo, who seemed to be far ahead now as she ran full speed through the field, backtracking toward the border of where the grass met dust. Surprised by the sight of her leaving, I turned around to see the man we had seen earlier, picking fruit. He was standing merely feet away from me, his face twisted into a scowl. My eyes widened. There were two others coming up behind him, and I saw others still hurrying to see what was going on. I was going to be trapped if I didn't do something quick, but my feet seemed glued to the ground, my stomach feeling as if it had just lurched into my throat. My hands fell to my sides, releasing my shirt and making the beautiful fruit roll out and smash onto the ground in front of me. I stared down now as the juice spilled, its color a deep red, like luscious blood seeping into the dirt below.

"Run, Anna!" Jo screamed.

Staring at the crowd gathering before me, I turned around and attempted to sprint away from the field and toward Jo. I could hear footsteps right behind me, but I didn't dare look back for fear that I would stumble. My only chance was to not make any mistakes. No tripping and no falling. I tried to keep focused on running, looking ahead toward Jo who stood safely in the distance. She was waiting for me. The knowledge that she wasn't leaving without me helped me gain determination to go on, even though my lungs felt as if they were about to explode and my legs seemed barely there, a mush of jelly threatening to collapse from underneath me at any moment.

A pain that took what little breath I had left crushed into my back to the right of my spine. White spots darted in front of my vision as I felt myself slip and go tumbling to the ground on my side. My back felt as if it was splitting apart, the pain now searing up into my neck. I managed to look back, and saw some young children running toward me, giant rocks held up in their hands. One of those rocks had just made a connection with the bones in my back. It appeared that I was about to be stoned to death.

Chapter 3

Panic settled in, as I didn't know where I was or what was happening. I tried to move my arms and legs, and then I felt the soreness of my back and remembered the rock hitting me. I winced in pain.

"Stop wiggling."

I looked up into the face of Jo. She was carrying me. "What are you doing? Set me down," I said.

She stopped walking and carefully placed me on my feet. I grimaced, but realized how fortunate I was to be alive. "Wow. How in the world are you strong enough to carry me? You're half my size."

"I've carried things a lot heavier than you," she confessed.

We were back in the dust, but I could see mountains towering above us. They were dark and creepy without a trace of color or plant life. I sat down and tried to reach around and feel my back. "Is it bad?" I asked.

"You're going to have a nasty bruise for a long time," Jo replied. She peered up into the mountains for a moment. "There's a gash in your skin. I cleansed it and put a dressing on it made of leaves. You got lucky. No broken bones."

"What happened? Why were they throwing rocks? I mean, I know we were taking their food, but they could've hit me in the head and ..."

"Killed you, yeah," Jo said, finishing my sentence for me. "They would've."

"How'd we escape?" I had so many unanswered questions. I needed to understand what was going on here in Evadere. Things here weren't like

Earth, and they weren't adding up in my mind. I needed to have a general understanding of this planet so I could be more prepared next time. *Next time*, I thought and shuddered. I really hoped there would be no next time like that. I didn't know how many hits a body could take from a rock, but I didn't want to find out.

Jo sighed and sat down next to me. She handed me a fruit and bit into one of her own. "Here, take this."

I hesitated.

"Take it," she insisted. "You need to eat. It's okay. We're safe, for now."

I gave her an uneasy look as I lifted the fruit to my lips. It tasted as sweet and juicy as it appeared. I had no idea what it was, but it was delicious and soothed both hunger and thirst at the same time.

"Delicious."

She nodded.

"How am I still alive?" I asked.

"I came back for you."

"You reached me before they did?" I raised my eyebrows. It seemed impossible.

She nodded. "I'm very fast. Those contributors could never catch me. I was just hoping not to get a rock in the back before getting away with you."

"Thank you," I whispered, amazed that she cared that much to risk her own life in order to save mine.

She shrugged as I had obviously embarrassed her by exposing her kindness.

"Now what?" The words slipped out from my lips. I needed to know if she had some sort of plan for me. Was she going to just take me this far and leave me? I couldn't blame her if she did, but I prayed that she wouldn't. Evadere was a terrifying place. Foreign didn't even begin to describe how I felt here. I was absolutely sure that I wouldn't be able to figure things out on my own without getting into trouble. I really needed this little girl to help me.

Jo finished the fruit and wiped her sticky mouth with the back of her hand. "I'm not sure." She stared at me then. I felt like a vulnerable human, weak and desperate. She was small, but so strong.

She had carried me this entire way. "I'm a Scave. I have to return to them. They'll be expecting me."

"And you can't take me with you?"

She cast her eyes toward the ground and shuffled her feet in the dust. "It's not an easy decision. I like you, Anna. I know you're lost here. I know I'm not like the other Scaves, too. They're not tolerant. When they know you're a human, they'll kill you. If they know I even helped you, they may kill me."

I could see the pain I was causing her. She had a good heart, but it seemed as though mostly everyone else here did not. She wanted to help me, but not at the cost of her life.

"Do you have to go back soon?" I asked.

"Yes."

"Can we just talk for a little while? Would that be okay?" I tried to remain calm, even though inside I was screaming at the top of my lungs for her to take me along with her. Night was settling in fast, and I didn't have any desire to be alone, afraid that the next thing that stumbled upon me would actually be a real monster and not at all someone like Jo.

"You probably have a million questions. Do you want to know about the contributors?" she asked.

"I saw that man touch the wilted plant. I saw it come back to life instantly."

"Of course," Jo said. "That's his contribution. That's his power."

"To bring life to sick plants?"

"To maintain all plants bearing food, so that the plants will flourish and produce more. They also pick all the food and store it in places like that building we hid behind. Then they send it out to the other contributors," Jo explained.

I took the last bite of my fruit, my stomach eagerly wanting more. I tried to shake the hunger pangs away. "So how do the powers work?"

"They're born with it. It's how this entire planet works. You're only born with one power, and that determines where you end up living."

"So all of those people back where we just were, all of them have the same power and they all contribute to the food?"

"Right," she said, happy that I was understanding a little. "Their offspring may not have a power to do that, but whatever power they have, that's where they go and learn how to use it to benefit others.

That's why the ground goes from green to gray. It's the boundary of where their power ends. They aren't using the gray parts for farming, so that part is left untouched."

"How many contributing groups are there?"

Jo looked up at me. "I'm not sure exactly. Hundreds."

"Really?"

"I've not seen them all, of course, but the Scaves have always stayed as close as possible to the farming contributors in order to keep fed."

"Scaves ..." I let the word linger momentarily. "You're a Scave?"

She nodded.

"And what does that mean exactly?"

"Scaves are just short for scavengers. We're misfits. We have no powers. We cannot contribute."

"Oh," I managed to get out. All of this talk about powers and whatnot and I hadn't even thought about someone not having a power.

"See?" Jo pointed out. "You're looking at me like I'm a misfit, now that you know I have no power."

"I'm sorry," I whispered. "I'm just processing it all."

"That's how everyone survives here, on powers from themselves and from others. Every once in a while, someone is born powerless. Aren't people like that back on Earth? Is everyone born the same?" she asked.

Earth. The word hit me like a brick, and I instantly wished I was there. I actually missed that place; my world. Here in Evadere, I was nothing. Others were trying to kill me. Here I was, a Scave, and then the realization of all poor little Jo probably had to go through in order just to survive came to me. "No," I said, choking a little from the sadness that washed over me. "Not everyone is the same.

There are misfits there, too, depending on how you view a misfit to be."

"Well, you don't have to pity me," she said in a hurt manner. "It's not like I'm alone."

My eyebrows raised in curiosity.

"Yeah, there's a group of us; actually a pretty large group now. But Scaves are … different."

"You just said you're different because you have no powers."

"Right, but I mean other than that. Scaves live up there, in those rocky cliffs. We hide up there from the contributors. We come out at night to take what we need, when we need it. We have to forage the land, and many of the older Scaves have become vicious. They've been hunted all their lives."

I shifted my position as the ache in my back was beginning to throb. Jo saw my discomfort and gave me a small smile.

"It's fine," she assured me. "Your back, I mean. I made sure it was cleaned out. There shouldn't be an infection as long as you keep it clean now."

"Thank you for that," I whispered. "Thank you for everything."

Those words seemed to uplift her spirits slightly. "A long time ago, when someone was born powerless, royalty killed them."

"Royalty? Like a king and queen type of thing?"

"Yeah," Jo said. "There's a queen here with a castle and everything. I've never seen it, though. It's the farthest from the farming contributors actually, but I've heard stories about it. And they got rid of the misfits because they couldn't contribute to society. Mothers began hiding their babies when they knew they were powerless, and eventually a small group of Scaves began living in these mountains together. They hate the royalty. They have been trying to get a group together large enough to wipe them out, to avenge the deaths of the other baby Scaves that were never given a chance to live. It's

been an ongoing battle between contributors and Scaves."

"The Scaves, your people, have to steal food and everything else you need from the contributors because you can't get it on your own, is that right?" I questioned her.

The sky grew darker, the stars larger. It was the same wondrous sky that I first laid eyes upon when Emry accidentally transported me to this world when he was back in the prison. The memory pained me.

"I don't think of it as stealing," she snapped defensively. "What you humans do on Earth is stealing.

We have every right to partake in that food as everyone else. It's wrong that they exclude us."

"I agree," I replied quickly. I wondered how much she knew about Earth. It seemed as if she knew a lot. She had a disgusted tone of voice when speaking about humans, and I didn't want to upset her. I didn't want to chase her away and leave me here all alone.

"Why do you think your people would want to kill me? If they hate how others tried to kill them, why would they want to kill others?"

Jo sighed. "They don't kill their own. They kill those that oppress them, which is mainly everyone else other than their own. You are not a Scave."

"Technically, here I sort of am."

"You are a human."

"You seem to know an awful lot about my kind," I admitted, trying to pry just a little to see how far I got.

She nodded. "I do. We all do. It's a shame that it's as they say, and you know nothing about us. I've had to explain all of this to you. You have no clue, do you?"

I stared at her curiously. I wasn't quite sure what she was getting at. "No," I mumbled.

"Listen," she said. "I'm tired. You're tired. We both need to rest. Let's just sleep here for the night and let me think about this whole thing a little while longer."

I was relieved, yet a little scared at the thought of another night in Evadere. The first one had been creepy enough. "Okay. Where do we sleep? Here?" I looked at the bare ground beneath us. It was hard, and I'd be covered in the dust.

The question had annoyed her. "Yes, here."

I watched curiously as she laid down in the gray filth and curled up on her side into a ball. There was nothing else around to even try to make a bed out of, so I just plopped down near her and closed my eyes. I was exhausted and my entire body hurt, especially my back, but the thoughts of how this was going to end up with me stuck here kept edging its way back into my mind.

My once heavenly realm, Evadere, now seemed to lurk with the threat of death around every twist and turn. I thought about the beach and Emry. As I wiggled my fingertips into the gray ashes below me, I struggled to find our love in this place. Surely Emry belonged here because of his power, but what exactly would his contribution be, and how did he come to be raised on Earth? I began to wonder if there were other planets out there that I had no clue about. Why did Earth seem so confined to just itself, and yet Jo seemed to know about where I was from?

My head hurt from all the "what ifs." I felt as though a train was ripping through me. Emotionally and physically, this place daunted me. All I had to depend on was Jo, a Scave with a big heart. At least, I hoped I could depend on her. Surely she wouldn't have gotten me all this way to lead me straight into a death trap with the other Scaves. I immediately shook the thought from my mind. No, there would be no reason for that.

She could have allowed the contributors to stone me to death instead of risk her own life to save mine. She was a good person, maybe the only good person by the sounds of it.

Oh, Emry, please come for me; find me, somehow, someway.

Chapter 4

For the next hour, I sat next to a too quiet Jo, the morning light edging its way up on the horizon. A throbbing ache from my wound reminded me it was still there, though it was bearable. I couldn't help but keep wondering what it was exactly that Jo was thinking. It unnerved me the way she was positioned, her head resting on her crossed arms as she stared off into the distance.

"They sent me to look for you, Jo."

My head snapped around to see who had snuck up on us. A teenage boy with protruding ribs and dark disheveled hair cut unevenly, peered down at me, an amused smirk on his lips as he pointed the end of a jagged spear at my head.

My eyes then shifted toward Jo, who sat parallel to me, her eyes large in fear at the sight of the strange boy. She quickly moved in front of me so that the weapon was now aimed at her. Puzzled by her reaction, he retracted the spear and lowered it to his side.

"What are you doing?" he snapped. "Why are you protecting this contributor? Why is she not tied up?"

I felt my pulse begin to race as Jo seemed so utterly terrified of this young man that she couldn't even find the right sense to speak.

"What are you up to, Jo?" He eyed her warily.

"Please, Rooney," Jo finally managed to say. "Leave her be."

"Why?" he asked, his hand tightening the grip around the spear still positioned at his side. "She's not a contributor," Jo mumbled.

"I ..." I began, feeling as if I needed to say something, anything to defend myself, but Jo held up a hand to my face, silencing me.

The young man glared at me, his cheeks flushing red. "Who is she, then?" he demanded to know.

Jo got to her feet and faced him. "She's a Scave."

The boy she had called Rooney immediately began to inspect my face. "How can that be possible?"

"It just is," Jo told him.

"She's one of us?" he asked, still a little uncertain.

"She's one of us." Jo's voice wasn't as shaky now. "Take us back with you?"

The boy's eyes were still locked on mine. I stayed very still as he examined me, feeling as though I was failing some sort of visual inspection.

"You have a lot of explaining to do," he said, his hand easing up on the weapon along with the rest of his body.

Jo nodded. "I know."

"Where is your sack of food?" he asked.

A wrinkle appeared in Jo's forehead. "I left it on the beach."

"How could you let that happen?" he yelled out, his temper flaring once again.

Jo looked back at me and then faced Rooney again. "I was trying to save her."

"You," he said, motioning toward me.

I tiptoed out from behind Jo and stood beside her. He looked so frail. I wondered why Jo was so afraid of him. He looked as though if hit hard enough, he'd shatter into a million pieces.

"You're a Scave?" Rooney questioned.

I glanced at Jo, who met my stare momentarily. "Yeah."

"What's your name?"

"Anna."

"I'm Rooney," he introduced himself. "What's your story?"

"It's a long one," Jo interrupted. "She's on the run from the contributors. It's not safe to stay here."

After a slight moment of hesitation, Rooney turned around and moved at a fast speed toward the base of the mountain. Jo and I exchanged glances one more time, and I understood that if I didn't go with them, I'd be left here alone to fend for myself. Either way, I had an uneasy feeling in the pit of my stomach. Wait for someone or something to come find me here by myself, or dive head first into the domains of the Scaves. I could also tell by the way Jo was acting, that these scavenger people weren't going to be the type to just accept me instantly when they laid eyes on me. I felt my hands tremble slightly. Taking a deep breath, I forced my legs to move and follow Jo and Rooney up the mountainside.

Long before I actually saw where Scaves lived, the smell of the place reached me. It reeked of body odor and feces, the combination strong and sour in my nostrils. I swallowed the impending vomit that made its way up my throat from the foul stench and paused for a moment to calm myself.

My palms fell to my knees as I hunched over and stared at the ground, a sudden lightheadedness coming on.

"Anna?" Jo turned around and headed back for me. Rooney was so far ahead; he was barely visible anymore.

"I'm okay," I mumbled. "Just a little sick."

"It's the smell, isn't it?"

I looked up at her. "It's awful."

"It's a terrible way to live, I know," she whispered. "But it's the way it is. We have nothing. We barely make it on our own, and we have no running water or anything."

"I'll suck it up. Just give me a minute," I promised, unsure if I believed myself.

"This isn't going to be pretty," Jo whispered.

"What do you mean?"

She sighed. "The Scaves are a gruesome people. Most aren't able to survive out here, but the ones that do, well, you'll see what I mean. I need you to remember something, though."

"What is it?" I asked, trying to continue to breathe through my mouth.

Jo turned around anxiously to keep an eye out for Rooney. He hadn't even noticed we had stopped following him yet. "Don't show too much of your mouth."

"Huh?"

"You know, your teeth."

"Jo!" Rooney called out in a musical tone, still far away.

I was making an attempt to process what she meant. All I could think about was that the Scaves were some sort of dog people who if shown another person's teeth, would think of it as a threat and immediately attack that person for having done so.

"We're coming!" she hollered back at him. "Just remember what I said," she added in a whisper. The small huts where the Scaves lived came into view first when entering their camp. They were made up of mismatched items, some wood, some bricks, finished off with rocks or leaves. It seemed whatever they had found, or took, was thrown together in order to make a shelter. The huts were very poorly made, and I wasn't going to dare go near the ones that had rocks as a roof, looking as though any wrong bump or movement inside or out could cause the whole thing to tumble down on your head.

"She's right here," Rooney shouted from up ahead.

He had obviously announced my arrival to the rest of them as I could hear the shuffling of feet dragging in the dust up ahead. My pulse sped up instantly. I took a deep breath and kept my head down as I trekked slowly on into the depths of the Scaves' realm. When I finally did look up, I gasped.

Jo had used the word gruesome. That didn't even begin to describe the appearance of these underfed, filthy people who now gathered around to see my coming. Rooney held out his arms and pointed directly at me.

"There she is," he announced. "Jo says she's a Scave."

My eyes met with a woman on my left, who only had one eye. The other side of her face was deformed and skin now mostly covered up the spot where her eye used to be. She didn't even bother to try to hide it. Her hair was gray, frizzy and long. The skin on her cheeks sagged. She reached out a very skinny arm toward me, as if to touch me. I uncomfortably moved out of her way so that she couldn't get close. I huddled toward Jo's side as I was eyed by even more Scaves. All of them turned to stare at me, their faces beholding curiosity filled with both concern and hatred at the same time.

Scave men had long hair and beards, some of them reaching their waists. Their collar bones protruded out from their shirtless bodies, and their skin was covered in the dust from the ground, as if permanently stuck there. A younger woman, probably in her 30s, drummed a long black fingernail along the side of her cheek as she examined me. I looked down at the ground. The smell of their unsanitary premises no longer bothered me. The fear of seeing the disgust in their beady, little eyes brought on a whole new, more overwhelming sensation that outweighed the previous one.

From the back of the crowd, an old man pushed his way through until he came to the front. He stood directly in front of me, his scraggly whitish-gray beard wrapped around his wrist. He held a crooked branch in the other hand as a cane to help prop himself up. The stench from his open mouth, which he breathed through, immediately made my nausea return as if something rotten was growing from inside his throat. He made a wheezing sound as he breathed, almost like a continuous growl. He had scars covering the skin on his face, and his teeth were sharp, the top ones overlapping his bottom lip in spots. He looked more like a beast than a man, far more horrific than any of the others. I clenched my fists at my side and swallowed hard.

"What are you?" he said, almost in a deep hiss.

It took every ounce of willpower I had not to run away right then and there. This was the kind of creature I pictured lurking on the banks of the Evadere beach at night when everything was black. This was a monster unlike anything my imagination could even have come up with, and yet here I was, standing in front of him, knowing this interrogation wasn't going to end well. I barely knew anything about contributors or Scaves. I could put some of the pieces together here and there and from what Jo had told me, but really, how was I going to pull this off?

I opened my mouth, but nothing came out. I clenched my hands together in front of me and looked at them. Licking my dry lips, I tried again. "A Scave," I whispered.

He made a disapproving groaning noise as he circled me now, looking me over. I felt as if he were my predator. He had to be some sort of leader of the Scaves, I guessed. "How is this so?" he questioned.

"I ..." Jo stuttered.

"Be quiet," he commanded her, holding up the stick to point in her direction.

Jo's head shot downward.

"Where did you find them?" he asked.

"At the bottom of the mountain," Rooney replied.

"Where were they coming from?"

"If I had to guess, it'd be near farming," Rooney continued.

"You're running from the farming contributors?" This ugly, frightening creature stood before me once again. One of his pointy teeth scraped against the bottom of his lip and a little drop of blood ran down to his chin. I watched in disgust as he brought up his arm with his beard wrapped around it and wiped it off with his hair.

"Yes," I whispered.

"Jo," he said in another growl, turning around. "Where's the sack?"

"She left it on the beach," Rooney answered for her. "It's gone."

A loud hissing noise came from the Scave's throat. Jo backed away from him. She was just as terrified of this *thing* as I was and she lived in a group with him. "What is your opinion on this matter?" he questioned Rooney, who didn't seem quite as juvenile while in the presence of his leader.

"I'm not sure I believe she's a Scave," Rooney told him.

The other Scaves from the crowd all grumbled in concern over my presence. "Were you sent by someone?" the man asked me.

"No," I said quickly.

"Perhaps by *royalty*?" He winced a little as he emphasized the word royalty, as if it pained him to say it and had to do so slowly in order to get it out. "Surely they wouldn't sacrifice their own to spy on us, unless they wanted you dead." He pressed his face closer to mine, and I felt my eyes water up from the rank smell protruding from his mouth.

"I..."

"I don't believe you!" he shouted before I could even finish.

A burning radiated down through the center of my chest and into my stomach. I took a few steps backward.

"You couldn't survive on your own all this time." He sniffed me, then gave me a look of pure disgust. "You're clean, healthy."

"Karn!" someone shouted out.

Everyone slowly turned around to look at two Scaves who had just entered the campsite, both of them appearing very similar to their leader, yet a little younger and stronger as they had more muscle built up. They looked just as hideous with their jagged teeth and long hair pulled back into a messy ponytail. They had two others with them, males, whose feet and hands were bound together with wire that had been placed on so tightly their skin was bleeding. Their mouths were gagged.

"You," the Scave leader snapped, pointing his staff at me. "Wait here. I'm not done with you yet."

He slowly limped over to where they stood. "What is this?"

"We found them hanging around the bottom of the hill," one said.

"They were alone," the other added, his voice huskier.

The contributors' eyes widened as they took in the sights around them. They appeared physically very *normal*, like a human. I wondered how long the Scaves had been on their own out here trying to survive. They were frail-looking from lack of nutrition, yet still had such a fierceness and determination about them.

How was I going to get out of this? I couldn't stay here and pretend to be a Scave. I was lost in this strange world and mingling with creatures I didn't know the first thing about. I had nowhere to turn as the certain doom awaiting me began its overwhelming descent upon my mind, impressing its hideous ideas into my imagination of the terrible things that I was going to have to endure here with the Scaves. Perhaps the contributors would see that I looked more like them, and I could talk some sense into them. Surely someone somewhere could tell me how I could get back to Earth, or point me in the right direction of someone that knew.

Karn let out a hissing sound, mixed with a growl, as he looked the contributors over, sniffing them as he got his face very close to their bodies. "What do you have to say for yourselves, contributors?"

One of the captives' head shot backward at the odor coming from Karn's mouth as a Scave removed his gag.

Karn let out a satisfied chuckle at his intimidation over these poor men before him.

"Who sent you?"

"We were just looking the land over."

"Why?"

The contributor and his friend exchanged nervous glances, which infuriated Karn as he poked the contributor with his staff. "Don't make me repeat myself," he warned him.

The contributor looked as if he were going to cry. "For the possibility of a new beginning there," the man stammered.

"Which group?" Karn pressed on.

"Water," the contributor answered quickly.

Karn looked up at the other Scaves who had brought the captives to him. He squinted his eyes making his entire face wrinkle. "You're lying."

"No," the man cried. "I'm not."

"She sent you, didn't she?"

The contributor raised his eyebrows, not understanding.

"Don't play stupid with me," he roared. "The queen. She sent you to spy on us, to see what we're up to."

"No..."

"You expect me to believe that water contributors would live so close to us? That's absurd," Karn went on. "No, you're a liar. She's getting scared, which means ..."He looked up, satisfied by some idea that had just entered his mind. "He's nearby." He got lost in his thoughts momentarily before looking back at the contributors. "Get rid of them," he ordered.

The Scave men grabbed hold of the contributors, who cried out. What were they going to do; kill them? Surely the Scaves would have pity, knowing that royalty used to kill them and hadn't turned into killers themselves.

"Please!" one of them begged. "Don't hurt us. We're telling you the truth. We wouldn't spy on you.

We don't even know the queen."

"Have mercy on us," the other squealed.

"Mercy." The word rolled harshly off Karn's tongue. He grinned, exposing his jagged teeth further, most of them blackened with decay. He placed a finger up to his chin, amused by whatever it was that was going on inside his twisted head, the beard still attached to his wrist as it was raised. "Perhaps we will have mercy on these two contributors. We'll give them the benefit of the doubt."

Jo glanced my way and gave me an uneasy stare. I lowered my eyebrows at her and then returned my attention to Karn.

A Scave woman joined the crowd now, carrying an elderly woman in her arms. She dumped her ruthlessly onto the ground. The woman groaned in pain as she made an attempt to sit up. I instinctively rushed over to the poor, old woman, and got down on my knees to help her up.

"Are you okay?" I whispered.

The sickly creature extended out thin arms and pushed me away from her. She moaned some more, but then was able to get herself into a sitting position. I assumed she was paralyzed by the way her legs were wasted away and limp at her side.

"Who is she?" the woman shouted. "Get her away from me."

I quickly backed away, realizing that everyone's eyes were on me. "What are you doing?" Jo asked angrily.

"I thought she was hurt," I replied, feeling color rush to my cheeks.

Jo glanced toward the old woman. "Of course she is. She's dying. Leave her be."

The paralyzed woman seemed like she was in such agony, yet still had that ferocious beast of being a Scave within her. This was a glimpse of poverty in another world. These people couldn't contribute and so they were considered useless, meaningless, and left for dead. The ones that did escape had to forage for what little food and water they could. They had to steal in order to survive. And medicine, I assumed, was nonexistent to these cave-like creatures. It was really no wonder that they were as fierce as they were. They were true survivors, even living off a land that flourished with absolutely nothing where they stayed. I couldn't even begin to fathom how lonely Evadere must be for them.

"Are you going to tell the others what you saw?" Karn asked the two captive contributors, who were still terrified standing before the revolting Scave.

"No," they both quickly answered, their voices quivering.

Karn exhaled loudly. "Very well, contributors," he finally said. "You may go. Release them so they can go home." He turned around and met glances with Rooney, who pressed his lips together tightly.

The other Scaves cut the wires away that had been binding the contributor's arms behind their backs. They made grunting noises as if dissatisfied with Karn's decision to set them free.

"Thank you," one of the contributors stammered.

"What are you waiting for?" Karn asked him. "Go."

The two men scrambled almost directly into each other before turning to leave. They started off walking nervously at first, then went into full sprint after a couple of yards. I wished that was me, able to get away from this intimidating group, able to have somewhere to go back to. Part of me sympathized with the Scaves as I could understand why they were the way they were, but the other part of me feared their ferociousness. Then again, Karn had just let those contributors walk away. Maybe he wasn't as bad as he seemed.

A sudden squeal like one made by an injured animal sent a burning sensation through the middle of my stomach. I looked out toward the two contributors as one had collapsed to the ground, a spear piercing his torso. The other contributor's speed was now halted by the shock of seeing the now dying man by his side, blood pouring out all around him as, within seconds, he went from his knees to lying on the ground, dead.

A shrill scream escaped from my throat as Jo hurried to silence me by throwing her hand over my mouth. Rooney stood perched atop a large rock positioned on the side of the path, another spear in his hand. The contributor looked at the dead man and then looked up at Rooney in horror. He held his hands up in surrender, his feet stumbling backward a little.

"Please!" he cried out. "Please, no ..." Before he could finish, Rooney had thrown another spear. It zoomed through the air in perfect alignment with the contributor pleading for his life before making contact with his forehead. A stunned look appeared on his bloody face before falling forward in the dust.

The thud of his body against the hard ground sent me spiraling around in a circle as I now hunched over on all fours puking up what little fruit I had eaten, the once sweet juice soured by my stomach acids as I hurled it all back up, tears streaming down my face. How could I have possibly just felt sorry for the Scaves only moments ago? I had just witnessed the cruelest thing I had ever seen. Karn had told them they were free to go. He made them think they were able to return to their homes. Now I understood what that glance had meant that had been shared between Karn and Rooney. He wanted Rooney to kill them. The Scaves' hatred toward the contributors was limitless.

"Get their bodies," Karn instructed the two Scave men who had brought the contributors in. "Make sure nothing is wasted."

Were they now going to use the contributors' corpses as a meal? I wondered, my guts instantly repulsed once again as I bent over to throw up, merely dry heaving this time, saliva pouring from the edges of my lips. I listened to Karn's heavy steps as he made his way back over to where I knelt, the end of his staff sinking in the dust in front of me.

"Get up," he commanded.

I slowly made my way back into a standing position. I wiped my mouth with the back of my hand.

Weakness made its way through me as I felt as though I would collapse. I longed for a real meal and a real bed. I longed for Earth and the green grass of Seneca. A twinge of worry zipped through me at where Emry was now. He must be going insane without knowing where I was. I forced my head to move upward so I could look the ghastly beast in the eyes, praying I wouldn't become ill and go to the ground again, afraid I'd never be able to get back up.

"How is it that you're so healthy after all this time out here alone?" he questioned in a mocking tone.

I closed my eyes momentarily, unsure how I was going to respond. My brain didn't want to seem to cooperate with my lethargic body. I licked my lips, the taste of putrid vomit returning to my tongue. I smiled nervously at Karn.

He backed away for a moment, gasping.

I glanced back at Jo, whose eyes were glued on us. When I looked back to Karn, his beady black eyes burned in fury. What was happening?

"I knew it!" he roared out. "Did you see that?"

A Scave woman quickly rushed up to me and stuck her repulsive fingers in my mouth, jerking up my lip. I backed away and attempted to spit out the filth.

"What are you doing?" I cried out.

The woman grinned, revealing a mouth of rot, her gums sagging and covering up the majority of what teeth she did have. "Such a pretty mouth," she said, her voice high-pitched and shaky.

Karn nodded. "Straight white teeth."

My hand shot up to my mouth to cover it up. Why had I done that? I had mistakenly smiled. Jo had warned me not expose my teeth. Now I understood why.

"Another spy?" the woman asked.

Karn narrowed his eyes. "This one has to be in trouble. They sent her out here to die."

"Please," I said. I needed to plead for my life now. I had to think of something, *anything* to undo what I had just done.

"Get her!" Karn yelled.

I closed my eyes and cringed, waiting for the Scaves to capture me. Nothing was happening. Then the rustle of feet startled me into turning around. Jo had made a mad dash to get away, but Rooney was right behind her. He took a leap and tackled the poor girl to the ground. She kicked and thrashed, even bit Rooney to get him to release her, but he had his arms locked securely around her, his strength overpowering hers. She struggled for a few more moments and then gave up, succumbing to her sobs. Rooney began carrying her back to Karn.

"This really pains me," Karn announced. "A traitor among us when I thought we were one."

Rooney still held Jo in his arms. She hung her head in shame, her hair falling over most of her face.

"The contributors must've promised you things," Karn continued. "What are you getting out of this?"

Jo remained silent, her body limp in Rooney's arms, her head still cast downward.

"Ashamed, are you? Do you think I'm a fool?" Karn's voice was getting more intensely angry by the moment. "I took you in, raised you from a baby when *they* didn't want you. They left you for dead.

You're alive because of me, and now you turn on me, on all of us?"

The group of Scaves behind us glared at Jo. Their faces held no sign of sympathy. "What do you want me to do with her?" Rooney asked.

Karn scratched his hairy chin. "I never expected this to happen."

"Let them fend for themselves," the Scave woman with the shaky voice suggested. "See if they can survive on their own." A smirk played on her lips.

Karn looked from Jo, to me, and then back to Jo. I wondered what he was contemplating. I was terrified; my palms now clammy and wet. He exhaled loudly. "Very well," he finally said. The decision was made. "We'll let them go."

"Go?" I asked.

He nodded. "Yes, go."

Jo's head jerked up. I watched her look at Karn, who exchanged a glance with Rooney behind her. "No!" Jo screamed, wiggling her way away from Rooney and turning to face him.

They meant to kill us. We would have the same fate as the two contributors before us. I would never get a chance to gaze upon the wondrous face of Emry Logan ever again.

"You can't do this," Jo begged. "We're friends."

Rooney stared back at her, his usual cocky demeanor nowhere to be found. He didn't want Jo killed, and was even more pained to have to be the one commanded to do so.

Jo's hands rose to her cheeks where tears now spilled uncontrollably from her eyes. She hurried to wipe them away, afraid to show any weakness in this time of despair. "Please, Rooney. This isn't what it looks like. I'm not a traitor."

Rooney swallowed hard.

"Don't be foolish," Karn warned him. "Leave," he said sternly to us.

I grabbed Jo's hand and headed down the same path we had come in, the same path where the contributors had been brutally murdered only moments ago, their bodies already taken away, but their spilled blood left to cool in the dust. Jo yanked her hand away from me.

"We have to go," I paused to look at her terrified face.

"Go where? We're going to die."

"This is all my fault," I mumbled. "I need to tell Karn that I ..."

"Just let it be. He won't be convinced." Jo began to walk, her eyes still on Rooney, who trailed a little way behind us.

I didn't know what to do, what to say. It felt hopeless to do either, but I had to try to do *something*.

I didn't want to die. Not here, like this, trapped in a world, and being pursued by a Scave. My mind raced with panic. "What is he doing?" I whispered, not wanting to look back, afraid I'd see the spear headed for me.

"Still following us." Jo's eyes were glued on him.

"You have to talk to him once we're away from Karn's eyes."

"Rooney isn't a traitor. He'd never disobey Karn," she said with little emotion.

I continued to walk by her side, the hope that I was still walking and not lying dead on the road becoming more encouraging by the moment. "He didn't hesitate to kill the contributors. Don't you think he'd have done it by now?"

"He's letting it drag out as a punishment to me," she replied, biting her lip a little. "This is a game to him."

"Jo, listen to me, I saw him hesitate back there in front of Karn. You two are friends. That means something. He hasn't grown up with those contributors he killed. They meant nothing to him. You're different." My heart was pounding, as if I were running a marathon. I had to convince her to try.

"I can't believe this is happening." Emotion now poured from Jo as she gave into her fears and let the tears flow freely. "I just thought it'd be okay, you know?"

I stopped walking to turn to her. I put my hand on her thin shoulder. "Thank you for trying to help me. I know it means little now, but without you, I had no hope.

Jo took a few steps back so that my hand fell from her shoulder. She glared at me angrily. "I'm a Scave. I don't know what I was thinking. I don't know why I can't be like the rest of them."

"Cruel?" I whispered. "You want to be like that? You can't be serious."

"My own mother abandoned me," she screamed out. "Why do I feel sad for her? I should want her dead. I shouldn't have followed you back at the beach. I should have moved on. I'm weak. I've always been a weak Scave."

I narrowed my eyes. "It's not a bad thing to be kind to someone else." I watched her intently, as she watched Rooney. Then I saw her eyes grow large in terror, and I knew that I'd soon be dead. I watched her mouth drop open. I didn't want to look, knew I shouldn't, but I did. I turned to see Rooney in the distance, a sharp spear in his hand, raised above his head and aimed directly at us.

Chapter 5

"Get up."

I was hunched over in the dust, my arms curled around my knees and my head bent down.

"Pathetic."

I dared to look up. Rooney was standing in front of me, the spear put away behind his back. I looked over at Jo, who was in a similar position as me.

"Cowards," he said, his voice sharp with anger, but I knew it was more at himself than us. He had spared our lives.

"Why didn't you go through with it?" Jo asked.

"I still can, if you want me to," he threatened.

I stood up and dusted off my legs. I swatted at my hair that was now hot and sticking to my neck.

Jo eyed him curiously for a moment. "Rooney, I'm ..."

"Shocked?" He glanced nervously behind him. "Me, too."

"But you can't go back now either," she said, still composing herself.

Rooney massaged the back of his neck with his hand. "Obviously."

Jo now looked my way. I raised my eyebrows, just as surprised but so grateful that Rooney had had a heart. When I had seen the spear raised, I went straight to the ground to await my fate but not wanting to see it coming.

"So, what now?" I asked, uncertain if I should speak or not as the guilt swelled within me knowing this was all my fault.

Rooney glared at me. "Are you a contributor?" Then he held up his hand and shook his head.

"Never mind. I expect answers, honest answers."

I nodded.

"But not now. Karn is going to send his two buffoons in search of me soon if we don't get going.

They'll kill us all." He ran down the path, Jo at his side. The weakness of everything that had happened still lingered, weighing me down, but I forced my muscles to move so that I could run, too, albeit behind them. I knew this was going to be physically demanding in every way, but I had to keep up or I'd be left behind. I doubted that Jo was going to be as sensitive with me this time.

By the time I caught up to Rooney and Jo, my lungs felt as if they were going to catch on fire within my chest. I felt as if I would throw up again, but I knew it would be dry heaves as there was nothing left in my stomach. I collapsed on the ground and took deep, giant breaths.

"Get her up," Jo said sternly to Rooney. "It's no good to lie down after a run like that."

Rooney put my arms around his neck and helped me into a sitting position. I lowered my head between my knees and hoped no dust would be sucked in my nose to add to my misery.

"Wow. Where is she from? She's so out of shape."

Jo knelt down beside me. She lifted my head to get a look at my eyes. "You alright, Anna?" I made my best attempt to nod.

She stood back up. "She's human."

"What?" Rooney took a few steps back, as if I were poison. "You're joking, right?"

"No."

"Where did you find a human?"

Jo crossed her arms as I felt my pulse begin to calm down a little and I was able to look at both of them without seeing white spots dart in my field of vision. "At the beach. She's lost."

"I've heard of them, but I've never seen one before."

"First time for me, too," Jo admitted.

"You can stop talking about me like I'm some sort of alien." I realized what I had just said, and all three of us burst out laughing.

"How did you get here? Well, I mean, you had to transport, but humans can't transport, can they?"

Rooney asked.

I rubbed sweat from my forehead, smudging dirt as I did so. "No, someone else transported me." Rooney and Jo exchanged worried glances. "What is it?" I asked.

"As far as we know," Jo began to explain. "The only ones that can transport are royalty."

"They have extreme powers," Rooney added.

"Meaning?" I raised my eyebrows.

Rooney rolled his eyes. "They have all the contributors' power plus their own. They can basically do anything. You don't know much about our world, do you?"

I made a failed attempt to get to my feet and sat back down.

"Just rest for a minute," Jo suggested.

"Why would I know anything about your world? In fact, how would I know anything about it?"

He looked at Jo again. "Then it's true what they say about humans."

She shrugged.

"How do you know about humans?" I snapped. "And what exactly do they say about humans?"

"That you're a selfish creature," Rooney replied.

Jo frowned. "That your world refuses to acknowledge the existence of others, other than your own."

I didn't know what to say. I supposed that was a true statement. I had thought the same thing when I had first found out about Evadere. Why didn't it seem like anyone else knew? Who had been hiding this world, keeping it a secret?

"Are there other worlds besides this one?" I asked.

Rooney and Jo met each other's gazes again. It was beginning to irritate me.

"Are we safe here?" Rooney asked her.

Jo took a look around. "For now, I'd say so. I doubt they'll find us for a while. We can rest. She really needs a break."

"Don't you exercise on Earth?" Rooney asked.

I gave him a mean glare. "Of course we do. It's just … I don't make it a habit of running for my life every day like it seems I've been doing here. I usually don't exercise on an empty stomach or after being scared half to death, either."

"Welcome to Scave life." Jo put her hands on her hips and continued to look around. "What are we going to do, Rooney?"

He sighed. "We have to find food and water, that's for sure. I'm parched."

"Anna's going to be dehydrated soon if we don't do something." She turned to me, but spoke to

Rooney. "Do you think we can make it out here on our own?"

"Haven't we always basically been on our own?" Rooney stated. "I mean, I've felt like I've been Karn's slave my whole life, really."

"Yeah," Jo agreed. "Anna, what is it you want to do?"

I leaned back on my arms and extended my legs straight out. A picture of Emry's face immediately entered my mind. I had to get back to him. I had to find a way. "I need to get back home. I can't stay here."

"We don't know how to transport back to Earth," Rooney said.

"No," Jo continued. "But we know who can, and we can take her there."

"You really do want to get killed, don't you?" he snapped. "If anyone hates us, royalty is at the very top of the list."

"Do you have something better to do?" Jo asked him. He looked hurt by the remark. "I'm taking her to the castle."

"You don't know how to get there," he reminded her.

"I'll figure out a way."

Rooney glanced at me, but spoke to Jo. "But I saved your life."

"And I'm paying you back by leaving you behind so you won't get killed at the castle," she told him.

A smirk played on my lips. Jo really was willing to help me after all I'd put her through. Maybe she was more like the old me, the one that needed a fresh start, to get away from her old life that did nothing but bring her down. She needed to get away from the Scaves and live how she wanted, no one to stop her. She stood up and started walking away. I immediately got up and followed. At least she was going at a much slower pace this time.

Rooney stayed behind for a few moments. I glanced back at him and then turned around, facing forward.

"Wait up," he called out. "I'm coming, too."

By the time night rolled around, I was nestled in soft leaves that Jo had brought me. We were near a small brook that they assured me was safe to drink from. I had bent over and cupped water into my mouth for what seemed like an hour before my thirst was satisfied. Rooney had run off for a while and brought back some sort of meat. I wasn't sure what it was, but I was in no position to be picky. It was a small amount, but I felt myself consuming it as if I were starving. I *was* starving and had exerted myself to the point of mere exhaustion. I couldn't even begin to comprehend all the frightening events I had experienced in the last two days. It was all like a bad nightmare that seemed all too real. Rooney and Jo sat there and watched me curiously.

"What?" I asked with a full mouth. I wiped my mouth with the back of my hand and waited until I had swallowed. "Aren't you two going to eat? Aren't you hungry?"

"We'll be okay," Jo informed me. "We're used to going days without eating."

"Yeah," Rooney added. "Looks like you're not, though."

I started to feel bad again. I was so hungry, and yet these two had gone and stolen food just for me, brought me here just to be comfortable and have water, and weren't partaking in the food. Humans were selfish, I thought. We eat three times or more a day and sometimes complain about that. They go *days* without eating? The fact that their bodies were used to such a thing was utterly astonishing.

"So, you mean you're not even hungry?" I asked them, shoving another bite of meat into my mouth.

"Not too bad, really," Jo replied. Rooney snickered.

Everyone took a moment to relax. We were on the outskirts of some contributor ground. In the distance stood large, shiny buildings, almost like skyscrapers except they had no windows. They were beautifully made in perfect rectangles reaching toward the red sky.

"Do you think we're okay here?" Rooney asked, in a whisper now.

Jo lay down on the ground and put her hands behind her head. "They never come out of their city." "Where are we?" I asked them.

"Iron contributors," Rooney answered. "Pretty neat, huh?"

I nodded, leaning over to get another drink of water, the coolness refreshing and easing the pain of my still scratchy throat. "So they make buildings?"

"Right," Rooney said, sounding sarcastic as if it were such a simple thing to comprehend. "They're mean when they do come out." He looked over at Jo, who lifted up her leg to expose a huge scar in the back of her calf.

"What's that from?" he asked.

"A contributor came after me with a pitchfork."

"It looks like it was a nasty wound," he remarked.

She nodded and rested her leg back down on the ground.

"I've never been this far myself, but I've heard stories about the iron contributors. I have to say, it's a pretty amazing place."

"Every place is amazing when it's not up in the mountains with the rest of the Scaves," she remarked.

I glanced over at her. She really was using this as a scapegoat to get away and had gotten to take Rooney, one of the strongest Scaves, with her.

He sighed. "Just because you're away from them, doesn't mean you're not still one."

"Yeah," she said, as if not caring. She closed her eyes.

Exhaustion set in as my belly felt better, my thirst quenched. My eye lids drooped.

"I can't believe you're a human," Rooney said.

"I can't believe I'm here. I can't believe that you were sent to kill me, and yet I'm going to have to trust you while I sleep tonight," I said.

He grinned.

"I'm still trying to figure this all out," I told him.

"What's that?" he asked.

"This world. I mean, if royalty have their own special powers plus everyone else's power, why do they even need the rest of the groups of contributors?"

He thought for a moment. "All I know is what Karn's told me. I didn't tend to ask him a lot of stuff, but from what I can gather, it would be too much work for royalty to do it all. They have the ability, but they need everyone else to function in order for them to live as royalty should live." He began chewing on a fingernail.

"Jo told me she was abandoned as a baby. What happened to you? I mean, you don't have to tell me if you don't want to…"

"The same thing basically." He shrugged as if not caring, but I could tell talking about this did cause him pain. "Left for dead by my father."

"And your father was a contributor?"

"Yeah."

"How were you found?"

"Scaves are rare. There aren't too many of us. From what I was told, a long time ago when a baby was born powerless, they were immediately taken to royalty and killed right away. Somewhere along the line, one contributor had a baby that they actually cared for and didn't take the baby to royalty like they were supposed to. She was able to hide him for a couple of years until someone else figured it out. She knew royalty was coming for him, so she let him go off by himself, hoping he'd be able to survive on his own."

"Was that Karn?" I asked.

"Yeah," he replied.

"Wow," I mumbled. "Do you know what happened to his mother?"

"Royalty took her away. I'm sure they killed her. She had broken a law. Contributors don't break laws, or they're severely punished. They're afraid of royalty. They obey them, even if it means getting rid of their own child."

I tried to let all of that settle in my mind. It gave me chills just thinking about how everyone lived on Evadere. At least humans think life is precious, don't they? Then I thought of all the wars being fought, people killing people, and I began to second guess myself.

"So they used to be killed, newborn Scaves," he went on. "After the Karn incident, it must've been looked down upon just to murder them, so they decided it would be better if they just got rid of the child, like they would no longer have the blood on their hands."

I could feel the meat churning in my stomach. I had eaten too fast, and this information disturbed me.

"They just throw the child away, leaving them for dead, abandoning them, and it's usually near the base of the mountain. Karn usually finds them, tries to help them. Some make it, some don't. It's a rough life from the start."

"I can see that," I said.

He looked at me as if slightly offended.

"Are there babies back there with the rest of the Scaves now?" I felt a sudden worry for them.

"No. Actually, Jo was the last one. It's been awhile. Either they're taking them somewhere else, killing them again, or there just haven't been any more born," he said.

"I don't get it," I said a little louder, my temper flaring. "They consider you a misfit only because you don't have a power? That's ridiculous."

"It's the way it is." He looked down to the ground, his toe stirring the dirt. "Are there misfits on Earth?"

I hesitated for a moment. It was the same type of question Jo had asked. Earth seemed so far away, unreachable really, and truthfully it really was right now for me. I thought of Seneca and the prison where I first saw Emry's face. "Yes, I suppose."

He eyed me for a second, but didn't bother asking anything more.

"What is it about Karn, then?" I asked. "What makes him such a ...?"

"Monster?" Rooney chuckled. "Well, he's been around the longest, has seen it all, has felt the wrath of the contributors against him every day he's breathed air. History is that he was the one who killed the king."

"What?" I gasped.

"Yeah," he continued. "He's gone to the castle and made it inside. He murdered King Calan. There were other Scaves with him that night; only a few, but they were very strong back then. All of them got away, but over the years, all have died except him. Everyone says he's too stubborn to die until he does what he has intended to do all this time."

"Which is?"

Rooney gazed over toward the tall buildings, outside lights illuminating them against the now darkened sky. "He wants the bloodline ended."

"I'm not following ..."

Rooney sighed. "You sure have a lot of questions."

"I'm just trying to understand it all. I'm stuck here, so I might as well know everything I possibly can and know what's going on," I told him in my defense.

He swallowed. "Well, the ones with all the power are royalty, like I said before. Royalty destroy Scaves. If the royal bloodline is gone, there will no longer be royalty. Are you following?"

"Royalty gives birth to more royalty?"

"Yes. Royalty chooses a mate, a contributor, marries them, and the child they have is born with royalty power. So Karn destroyed Calan so he couldn't have children, so no more bloodline would exist."

"So why is he still after them?"

"Because," Rooney gave me another look as if I were a moron, "Calan married Atavia, a contributor, and Atavia had a son. Karn had intentions of killing both the prince and the king the night he attacked the castle."

"Oh," I said. "And he failed?"

"Right. Somehow, the baby prince was safely hidden. It's only a matter of time before he's revealed. Karn has hunted for him everywhere. He hunts for him every day. He gets no rest until he's destroyed him, too."

"So really, from what I can see, Karn isn't just taking in newborn Scaves and helping to raise them to be nice; he's building up an army against royalty. He's going to attack when the prince returns."

"I suppose it's something like that," Rooney said softly. "I'd like to think somewhere, deep inside, he cared for us, though. Then again, he did order Jo killed today."

"But he considered her a traitor," I reminded him.

He nodded. "Yeah, little did he know."

I laid back near Jo and stared at the sky. "I'm exhausted. I don't know if it's okay to sleep, but I need to."

"Don't think this conversation is over," he said. "There's more to your story, too, *human*."

I cringed slightly at his tone of voice and knew he wanted more information on Emry. Sleep came on too quickly to bother to care.

"Jo! Anna!"

I started to the alarmed voice of Rooney and sat straight up in panic. Everything was still dark and hazy, as it wasn't quite morning yet. I watched Jo rush over to his side, and they whispered amongst themselves for a few seconds. I stood up and plucked away leaves that were sticking to my skin. I sucked in a big gulp of air and waited impatiently for them to tell me what was going on. After a few moments, I decided to go to them.

"What is it?" I asked in a quiet tone.

"Are you sure?" Jo asked Rooney.

He nodded. "I'm telling you, I saw a contributor, and he's headed this way."

"Why were you so close?" she asked.

He shrugged. "Curious, I guess. I couldn't sleep. Doesn't matter. We have to leave. Now."

Jo put her hands on her hips. "They usually don't come out, but ..."

"Yeah, right," he said. "You're the one that said you got hit with a pitchfork here."

She gave me a worried glance. "True." She waited a few more seconds, her eyes scanning the bottoms of the buildings for movement. "Okay. Let's go."

We began to walk away from the silver line of the city and back into the unknown dusty paths of Evadere. I kept near Rooney and Jo's side, constantly glancing over my shoulder to make sure no one was sneaking up behind us with a pitchfork.

"Shouldn't we have gathered water or something?" I asked. "Since it was right there."

"With what?" Rooney asked.

"Yeah," Jo chimed in. "Do you have containers to put water in?"

"Oh." I sulked a little. Of course we didn't have anything with us. I was just so worried that we wouldn't be able to find more. Then again, I was with two scavengers.

"Do you feel rested at all?" Jo asked me a few minutes later.

"Not too bad, actually," I answered. I started to think about where we were headed next. I felt as if we needed direction, and I wasn't sure these two were on the same page as me. I didn't want to nag them, but it kept coming to the tip of my tongue. "So, where to next?" I hoped that didn't sound too pushy.

Jo ran her fingers through her hair and tossed it behind her back. "Well, I've been thinking about that."

"I'd like to hear this," Rooney said in a belittling manner. "What's your master plan for finding the castle?"

She pressed her lips together. "That's just it," she told him. "I don't think we can find the castle on our own. It's too risky to try. We'll be going into territory none of us are familiar with and putting our lives into serious danger."

"You haven't considered yourself in serious danger all this whole time?" Rooney asked smartly.

Jo ignored him. "Mostly all contributors hate us Scaves."

"No, *all* of them do," Rooney said.

"You'd think that, but one group isn't as bad as the others."

I lowered my eyebrows. When had Jo even had the time to think about all of this? I wondered.

Wasn't she just as exhausted last night and passed right out, too?

"Enlighten me, please," Rooney said.

"Every group of contributors has tried to kill me except one. Medical."

"Really?" Rooney ran his fingers along the tip of one of the spears he carried as we walked. "Do you know this from experience?"

Jo nodded. "I tried to steal medicine from them once. They're smart. They had nets set up, waiting to trap me. Instead of killing me, they actually gave me the medicine I needed. See, I figure they're this way because they save people's lives. They strive to preserve life, even if it means the life of a Scave."

"Interesting," Rooney said. "It does make sense. So say we do go and they don't kill us. Then what?"

Jo shrugged. "I'm not really sure." She glanced my way. "I guess since there's three of us, we need to make a big entrance, steal *a lot*. Hopefully we'll get captured."

"And?" I asked, curious where this plan was leading.

She flashed a nervous smile. "They'll take us to the castle as captives?"

Rooney sighed and crossed his arms. "Take us to the castle where we'll get killed."

The thought of going to the castle was intriguing. I wondered how accepting of me they'd really be, these glorified contributors.

"We have Anna with us; a human," she reminded him.

Their eyes turned to me, the alien. I took a deep breath, my nerves acting up.

"Yeah, and we all know how everyone feels about humans around here," Rooney said, sarcastically. "Humans are just as bad, if not more so than Scaves."

The label of being a human was haunting. Earth had this dirty reputation around here, and I seemed to be upholding the stereotype.

"Well," Jo said, her hands resting on her hips, "Anna is my friend, human or not, and she needs to get home."

Rooney stood there for a few moments, his mind processing the scheme at hand and all of the possible awful scenarios that could happen as a result. Even my own mind spun with all sorts of terrible things that led to death as I wasn't sure how I could get near, let alone trust, a contributor group to not kill us.

"Alright," he finally said. "Let's go get captured."

Chapter 6

"Are you ready for this?" Jo whispered.

I looked at the small Scave girl and thought what a coward I was compared to her. She was doing this all for me. She was getting nothing out of it. Oh, how I missed the normalcy of Earth, of being near Emry. Evadere was wearing on me. I was starving. I felt lethargic, as if I could just fall over. But I couldn't whine about any of this, not to Jo or Rooney. They had been abandoned by their birth parents, taken in by the monster Karn, and were true survivors by every sense of the word. They had to work for everything they ever had, which really wasn't much. They could die right now and their lives would matter little else to everyone here. They were cast away and forced to live rugged lives where life wasn't meant to be one to enjoy, but merely to keep breathing. I couldn't act like a spoiled human here. Not now. Not with them. Yet somehow these two cared more than the other Scaves. I wondered if it was because they were still young and not as damaged as the others, who seemed to be coldblooded and cruel, or maybe they were just smarter. They had become friends themselves and now with me, an outsider and misfit myself here. Their friendship was one of a loyalty I had never known before. All of our lives were in danger, and it was my fault that this was so, yet they were still eager and willing to try to help. They no longer even had a home, and yet wanted me to return to mine. I *was* being a selfish human. I did want their help, even though I knew it could cost them the one thing they valued the most, their lives. I was being selfish because I missed Emry Logan and we had just started our own world together before such a cruel separation. I had no one else to turn to besides Jo and Rooney. Without them, Evadere would consume me, and I'd never lay eyes on Emry again. It was an agonizing fate to even attempt to contemplate. I wouldn't accept that possibility. I had to keep trying. "Jo, it doesn't matter if you left me here for a week, I'd never be ready," I confessed. "Let's just do what we have to do."

She nodded. "Up there in the distance is where the medical contributors live."

I squinted my eyes, which were now burning from both the bright sun and the dust kicked up from following Rooney. I saw what looked like white tents, their open walls blowing gently in the breeze.

"This seems like such an idiotic plan," Rooney huffed. "We're just going to walk up to them and start taking their stuff?"

"Got a better one?" Jo asked.

He didn't reply.

"That big building on the far side," she pointed out. "That's the one that holds the largest amount of supplies. I was in there before." She turned around and grabbed my hand. "You okay?"

I swallowed.

"I wish I did have a better plan," she said. "This is the biggest entrance, though, going in the middle of daylight.

I nodded. "Jo, before we go ..."

She raised her eyebrows.

"I want to say thank you to you and Rooney."

"Don't be getting all soft on us, human," Rooney said sternly.

"No, really, Rooney," I continued. "It's my fault you're no longer with Karn."

"It was time to leave Karn," Jo said. "It's something I've thought about for a long time, just never had the guts to do."

"What?" Rooney seemed surprised. "You never told me that."

"How could I? You were like his little puppet," she said.

He looked hurt by her statement.

"This war thing," Jo continued. "Going on between him and royalty, it's bigger than me. It's something I've never been interested in being a part of."

"But they throw us away like garbage," Rooney interjected.

"I was born the way I was born. At least I'm still alive."

Rooney rolled his eyes. "Well, I don't feel the same way. I hate royalty. I'm going to make that known once we're at the castle, too."

Jo shrugged. "Good luck with that."

He glared at her.

"You have every right to be mad," I said. "What has been going on here with Scaves versus contributors isn't right. Something has to change. Rooney, you're a good guy. Don't let your anger change who you really are."

Rooney turned away from me and looked at Jo. "Are you ready then?"

"What's the matter, Rooney?" Jo grinned. "This emotional stuff too much for your manly heart to handle?"

He stomped off as both Jo and I burst into a fit of giggles.

Within minutes, we were walking onto the land where the medical contributors lived. The large white tent came into view. It was the largest of the buildings and its color an illuminating brightness.

We walked right up to it and stepped inside. There were contributors in there. Rooney and Jo separated, each one going the opposite direction in the supply tent. There were all kinds of bottles and different sizes of boxes, most of them stacked high and labeled. I trailed Jo.

I watched her grab bottles of medicine and stuff them into the bottom of her shirt now made into a pouch like she had with the fruit. Rooney did the same thing. There were three contributors that I could see. They didn't even seem to notice us. I ran my fingertips along the smooth glass of one of the bottles. I went to pick it up but then jerked my hand back. For some reason, I couldn't do it. I couldn't steal it. I had cold feet. This was all just a game to get to the castle. I glanced up. Where was Jo? My palms turned hot and clammy. I squeezed my hands into tight balls at the sides of my body. The contributors I had seen were gone, too. Then I heard a chilling scream.

Racing toward the noise, my heart pumped so fast it was as if I could feel it pulsating up into my ears. I felt ill as I made my way around a shelf and stopped dead.

In the corner of the tent lay Jo. A very burly, muscular contributor towered over her, a steel pipe clenched in his hands. I immediately wondered why Jo wasn't running. I knew she wanted to get caught, but this man was going to kill her.

"Jo." The word got caught in my throat and came out as a choked whisper.

Then the realization that she must be injured entered my mind. The contributor must have already hit her with the pipe. That was the only logical reason for her to still be in the position she was in.

A flash of movement caught my attention. Within seconds, Rooney was on the back of the contributor. He wrapped his thin arms around the thick neck of the contributor. He squeezed. The arms of the man flailed in the air helplessly by the surprise attack. Jo still lay on the floor of the tent, propped up on her elbows now, her face aghast as she watched Rooney attempt to battle the strong man.

Do something, I thought. Why couldn't I move? Jo said this was a peaceful contributor group, yet here was this horrific fight going on before my eyes, and I stood paralyzed, the coward I was.

The contributor's face was beginning to turn red. Maybe Rooney could pull this off and take him down. Suddenly, the contributor violently bent forward. Rooney was thrown from the man's back, landing on the floor of the tent with a hard thud. He laid motionless for a moment, stunned from the traumatic fall. The brawny man rushed over to Rooney and swung his arms backward, the steel pipe raised high in the air.

"No!" I heard someone behind me yell out.

It was too late. The steel pipe came down forcefully. It collided with the bone of Rooney's skull, crushing it to pieces.

I covered my mouth in horror. Rooney's leg twitched momentarily and then … nothing. I heard Jo cry out and cover her eyes from the gruesome sight of her best friend's head being brutally beaten in by a supposedly peaceful medical contributor. I collapsed to my knees, my eyes still locked on Rooney as if what I had just seen hadn't really happened, as if he would suddenly come back to life and jump up ready to battle again.

More contributors entered the tent. A woman hurried over to the man with the bloody pipe still locked in his hand as he angrily gazed down at the Scave he had just ripped the life from.

"Put it down," the woman cried, reached out for the weapon, and took it from him. "Leave them alone."

He turned around and gave her a hard glare. Then he stomped away and exited the tent. A younger male walked over to Rooney and gazed down upon him. He put his hands up in the air and looked at the woman, who wiped tears away from her cheeks before turning around to tend to Jo. Jo began to fight the woman, who knelt at her side trying to examine her legs. She flung her arms wildly in the air, trying to get the woman away.

"It's okay, child," the woman said in a soothing manner. "I won't hurt you. It's okay. Please, child."

I struggled to get to my feet again. I didn't even know if I had the strength to walk. I took two steps toward Jo before someone grabbed my arms and held them behind my back.

"Where do you think you're going?" someone whispered to me.

I glanced back into the face of yet another contributor, who now bound my hands with rope.

"Pick her up," he instructed someone else, gesturing toward Jo.

"She's hurt," the woman said next to her. "I think her leg's broken. Don't harm either one of them."

"I won't," he promised. "But royalty has already been contacted. They will be leaving soon. You can tend to her once she's properly tied and can't get away."

"Why did you call them?" the woman asked angrily, pulling on the skirt of her dress as she stood up to face him.

"You would rather they be set free?" he asked.

"That's right, I would," she replied.

He chuckled. "You would say something like that. You're a softy for the Scaves, even after they've tried to steal from us yet again."

"Their people get sick, too," she reminded him.

"They are hardly people," he replied.

The woman gave him another hard glare.

I tried to move my hands behind my back. Any movement made the rope dig into my skin deeper. I was forced to walk out of the tent as I glanced behind and saw them restraining Jo. Once outside, I stared up at the red sky before me. It was as if I were in the middle of a maze. It was so frustrating to be stuck here. My stomach churned from the image of Rooney's deformed, broken face as it popped in my mind at that instant, and I bent over and dry heaved forcefully. Saliva collected at the edges of my lips as I spit again and again onto the ground. When I stood up straight again, Jo was beside me, maintaining her balance on one foot. Blood dripped down the other leg, a gash below the knee. She didn't make eye contact with me, and I didn't know what to say, so I kept my mouth shut.

The contributor woman who had been inside the tent came out with an armful of things. She stood in front of Jo and commanded her to sit on the ground.

"Just leave it be," Jo snapped as the woman hurried to begin fixing Jo's wound.

"Now don't be foolish." She poured something onto the wound, and Jo cringed from the sting.

"That's a good girl. This will clean it out. We need to stop the bleeding fast."

The flap of the tent wall opened from behind and out came another contributor, Rooney's limp body in his arms. He tossed it carelessly down onto the ground beside Jo.

"Why did you do that?" the woman asked him in anger. "Get him out of here."

The contributor ignored her and kept walking.

I got a good look at Rooney now. I hated myself for looking and felt the muscles within my stomach clench once more.

Jo carefully took Rooney's hand in hers and held onto it.

The contributor woman sighed as she continued to clean up Jo's leg. "I'm sorry that happened to your friend there, child. I'm sorry that this has happened to your life."

Jo stared up at her for a brief moment, tears threatening to spill. She released Rooney's hand and turned away from him then, a sudden stubbornness coming over her as she refused to cry.

"Jo, I ..." I began to whisper. What was I going to say to her? What could I say? Rooney's blood was now on my hands. She had her leg gashed open because of me. This plan had turned into disaster, a life lost, and it had been all for me. I felt overwhelmed as if I no longer had an ounce of strength left in me to be able to face this place anymore. This was just too much to handle. I needed to give up and stay away from Jo before she ended up in the same position as Rooney. My heavy eyelids closed.

"They're here," someone said.

My eyes fluttered back open. A group of contributors hovered nearby, staring and speaking about us as if we weren't even there.

"What would you have us do?" one of the contributors asked a man who stood the closest to me. Our eyes met. He was well-dressed in silky white pants and a matching shirt with a gold-colored collar. His eyes left my face as he now looked to the lifeless body by my side. He sighed and put both hands on his hips. "Dispose of that body," he instructed them. "Are they contained?"

"Yes, sir."

"Good." He turned his back to us. "Get them some water and put them in the wagon." He then made his way through the people and disappeared into the crowd.

Two men hurried forward. One took hold of Rooney's arms, the other his legs. I turned my face so I wouldn't be able to get a glimpse of his crushed skull. Then a boy brought a cup of water and held it to my lips. It was cold and refreshing as it trickled down my throat. I felt better for the moment. I drank the entire thing, and then he ran off to get another cup full for Jo. We were pulled to our feet and I clumsily stumbled toward some sort of vehicle up ahead. Once inside, I sat down and leaned my head against the side of the wall of the wagon. Jo was across from me, and some more well-dressed contributors positioned themselves nearby to keep an eye on us. I felt the wagon lurch forward. I felt Jo's eyes on me, but I was too tired to be able to fight the exhaustion any longer. We were now captives, likely off to the castle. Their plan had been a success, yet we had lost Rooney in the process. The wetness of tears spilled onto my eyelashes. Then my eyes closed, and I finally slept. When I woke up, I knew we'd be at the castle.

Chapter 7

"Jo?" I whispered in the dark.

There was no reply.

"Jo!" I hissed a little louder.

"I'm here," her meek voice said nearby.

It was pitch black as I sat up on the cold, hard floor. I put both arms up and tried to search around.

There was nothing.

"Did we make it?" I asked.

"To the castle?" Jo said. "Yes. You've been sleeping."

I had slept through the entire trip to the castle, along with them bringing me in here. "We're in a dungeon," Jo added.

I cringed at the word. It made me feel even more worthless than I had before. I clenched my hand into a fist and then extended out my fingers. My joints were so sore. "How long have we been here?"

"Not long. A few hours at most," she answered. "I feel like we're waiting for something. I don't know."

I rubbed my temples as the beginning of a headache was forming. "What are you going to do?" Jo whispered.

It was up to me to get us out. I had to say something to the very next person that came in here. I had to be bold and tell them I was a human and that my being here was a mistake. I had to convince the royalty to somehow accept Jo also. This was going to get messy, I could feel it. It seemed that everyone here loathed humans just as much as Scaves.

A hint of light began to fill the room little by little as a heavy door opened on the opposite wall. I threw my hand in front of my eyes as they adjusted. Jo scampered across the floor and huddled near my side, nearly knocking me backward.

"Over here, your majesty."

"Where?"

"There. What would you have us do with them?"

"How many Scaves did you say?"

"Two, your majesty."

"I really don't know what to do ..."

"Get up," someone commanded.

I unshielded my eyes and stood, leaning over and offering a hand to help Jo stand also. She took my hand, and we walked over to the thick bars before us. I had to squint to focus on the two people within arm's reach on the other side of the bars. I could make out the form of a male contributor similarly dressed to those who had picked us up and hauled us here. Then out of the shadows another person stepped into sight. All fatigue instantly fled from my veins as I covered my mouth and gasped.

"Anna?"

"What ..." I stuttered.

Jo let go of my hand. I could feel her eyes giving me a questioning look.

I grabbed hold of the bars with both hands and pressed my face against it. "Is it really you?" Before me stood Emry dressed in a red gown, a white cloak on his back. He seemed equally as shocked to see me.

"Let her go. Now," Emry said in a very commanding tone.

The man at his side hesitated. "Your majesty?"

Emry's face burned as his temper flared. "Are you deaf? Let her out."

The man fumbled with his keys. His hand trembled as he finally found the correct one and unlocked the steel door. The moment he opened it, I rushed past him and practically leapt into Emry's arms. He stumbled backward happily as I wrapped my arms around his neck.

"Anna! How in the world ...?" He wrapped his arms around me as well and twirled me in a circle.

"I've missed you so much."

"Me, too," I whispered, tears threatening the edges of my eyelids. "Me, too."

Horrified by our sudden bonding, the contributor's face drained of all color. He just stood there for a few moments before shutting the barred door again.

Emry gave the man another glare before returning his attention to me. He placed me in front of him and put his hands to my face. His eyes became gentle as he looked me over. "What's happened to you? Are you alright?"

"You have no idea what I've been through. I never thought I'd see your beautiful face again." My brain hummed with all kinds of things I wanted, needed to say to Emry this very second. The adrenaline pulsated through me. This was just so unexpected. I thought I'd never experience this kind of joy again. Here he was, standing right in front of me. We were together again. I knew I'd be safe. My worries had vanished. The feeling was surreal.

"Come," Emry said, turning me toward the door that led out of the dungeon. He placed a hand on my back as he looked over his shoulder at the contributor. "Let's get out of here and go talk."

I nodded and glanced backward. Little Jo was still standing there, face pressed against the bars, dumbfounded by what she was seeing. "Wait."

Emry gave me a puzzled look.

"That's Jo," I told him, motioning toward the dungeon. "She's my friend. You have to let her out. I can't leave her here."

He hesitated for a moment, his eyes meeting the horrified look of the contributor.

"Emry, please," I pleaded. "She's the only reason I'm here. Without her, I'd be dead."

"Get her out of there, too," Emry instructed the contributor.

Jo grinned as she stepped away from the restraint of the dungeon and hurried to cling onto my arm, her eyes shifting curiously to Emry.

Emry led us up the stairs from the dark dungeon and into the brightly lit magnificent castle. The floors, walls, and ceilings were all made from cement with handcrafted designs of art etched into it. It was lined with luxurious, colorful furniture. I tried to take it all in, but my mind was still processing that Emry was here. He had no hesitation of where he was going as we walked up a shining spiral staircase with a very unique twisted rope railing. He turned abruptly into the first room on the right at the top of the stairs and pulled me in with him. The contributor had followed. Emry raised his eyebrows at him as he got ready to shut the door.

"But your majesty," the contributor said. "They're Scaves."

"No," Emry replied. "She's not." He slammed the door shut and turned to face me.

We were in some sort of study. The walls were lined with books and decorative paintings. Jo wandered about the room in amazement. Emry sat me down on a couch with velvety blue cushions. The sudden comfort felt heavenly. I put my head on Emry's shoulder and began to weep. I couldn't help it. I had felt as if I had been forced to be strong and keep all of my emotions inside all this time, and with Emry, my walls came tumbling down. I just hadn't expected such a happy ending to all of this Evadere madness. Emry lifted my head from his shoulder and stared into my soggy eyes. His own eyes held concern and a fierce anger.

I forced a smile. "Your majesty?" A chuckle escaped from my throat.

Emry smirked. "You don't know, do you?"

I shook my head. "All I know is that our once paradise, Evadere, is a place of pure hell."

"What?" He studied me for a moment longer. "I thought you were back on Earth. I thought you knew I was here and what was going on."

"Why would you think that?" I asked, now realizing he had never been worried about me. He hadn't even searched for me. "You left me on the beach. I thought you had gone back to Earth without me."

His eyebrows got lower. "My mother sent for me. She said you were safe and that everything had been explained to you."

"Your mother?"

He nodded. "My mother, the queen."

I gasped. "Queen Atavia?"

Jo glanced back from the news, concern filling her scared eyes. Then she continued to walk around, running her hands over top of a statue in the corner.

"You know her?" he asked.

"Only what the Scaves have said," I answered.

"How did you end up with the Scaves? How did you end up here?" His temper was flaring again.

I took a deep breath. "You left me on the beach," I repeated. "I couldn't transport myself back to Earth." I didn't want to explain. I wanted to know exactly what was going on here with him. "You're a prince?"

"I'm going to be king," he said, sticking his chest out a little as he did so.

"Well, now I guess we know why you can transport. Only royalty can do that, right?"

"I thought you didn't know anything," he said.

I rolled my eyes and grinned. "I've been all over this planet trying to survive, trying to find a way back to Earth, back to you."

"Are you hurt?"

"Not physically. Maybe a little emotionally from what I've witnessed the last few days. Did your mother explain to you what's going on out there with the contributors versus the Scaves?"

"They're dangerous," Emry quickly said.

"The Scaves?" I met eyes with Jo again, who kept her distance and just listened.

He nodded.

"Only Karn."

"You know about Karn?"

"Oh, yes," I told him. "I've met Karn."

"What?" He took hold of both of my hands as if he were never letting go again.

"He's mean, yes, but only because this world has warped him into becoming this gruesome beast who has had to survive without nothing his entire life."

"Anna, you don't know what you're saying. The Scaves are a horrible people. They're trying to kill me. They want rid of the blood line," Emry tried to explain.

I ran my fingers through his brown hair and traced the outline of his distinct jaw. "I was a Scave for a few days, Emry, and I couldn't imagine how terrible it must be to actually live as one for an entire lifetime."

He opened his mouth to interject, but decided against it. "I'm so sorry you've been through all this. I swear I had no idea."

"All I knew is that I had to get to the castle, that someone here would have the ability to get me home. I just didn't know how I was going to convince anyone here of why they would help me."

"Why wouldn't they?"

I frowned. "Because I'm a human."

He gave me a worried gaze again, as if trying to look through me to see what I had been through the last few days.

"Please," I said. "Tell me what's going on."

He closed his eyes for a moment, his hands still gripping onto my own. "Atavia is my real mother."

"So you said."

He nodded. "Right. She hid me on Earth when I was a baby, because the Scaves were after me.

They killed my father."

"Karn killed your father."

"Yeah, Karn. She didn't want to give me up, but she knew if I were to stay here, I probably wouldn't survive. She set up the entire adoption thing on Earth. Lainey Tritt was a discrete choice."

"Did Lainey Tritt know you were a ... prince?" The word stuck in my throat. Emry Logan was a prince of Evadere. I had always known he belonged to this world instead of mine.

"No, no. Anna, can I get you and your friend anything? Have you eaten? You look ..."

"Beautiful?" I laughed, knowing how disgusting I probably did look. It hadn't even entered my mind until he had mentioned it that he was looking at me in all of my filthy glory. "I do need to be cleaned up."

Emry stood, ready to command someone to draw a bath for me I'm sure.

"No," I said, pulling him back onto the couch. "I need to know everything. Please."

He took a deep breath and ran his fingers through his hair. As he looked down, the pieces of hair fell back down over his eyes. The familiarity of this habit of Emry's was wonderful.

"You're right. Okay. Ben Hanley, my so-called lawyer, is really my protector. He's watched over me on Earth since I was a baby and has reported my every move to my mother."

"Really?"

"Yeah. He came for me on the beach. My mother knew of all the trouble I had gone through on Earth with Mrs. Anderson, and she sent for me. It was time for me to come home, she said.

It was time for me to fulfill my destiny as king and deal with … things."

I knew he had meant to say the Scaves, but now sensed my sensitivity on the subject. "Mrs. Anderson, the witch?"

"She's from this world originally. She practiced black magic here. She was beginning to threaten royalty and became a hindrance to my mother, so my mother exiled her to Earth. Somehow, she found out about me there."

"Hmm," I said, this new information swarming around in my brain. "It's interesting about Earth." Emry raised his eyebrows.

"You know, Earth as a place to hide you and also a place of exile?"

"What are you getting at?"

I shifted positions on the couch. "What exactly does your real mother think about Earth, about humans?"

He rubbed the back of his neck and stood. He began pacing around the room. "You're right, Anna.

Earth is thought of as an area of waste."

"Humans, the lowly life form; lowly like Scaves?" I questioned. I suddenly felt the need to defend myself. I already felt threatened by his mother, the queen.

"Not lowly in the same way. Humans are thought to be selfish."

"So I've heard."

"They don't have any faith in themselves, in God. They don't believe in other life forms, other planets. Come on, Anna, this isn't exactly news to you. These things are all true about humans."

"I believe in myself, Emry," I said in a quiet tone. "I believe in God."

"You're an exception to the rule."

"Am I?"

Emry scooped me up in his arms. "Anna, I love you. I'd never let anything bad happen to you."

"Oh, really?"

Emry looked hurt by the comment.

"Do you know how many times others wanted me dead here? You didn't even know where I was."

He swallowed. "I'm so, so sorry. I know. I know. I don't know how things got so messed up. I was assured when I was approached on the beach that when you woke up, things would be explained to you; that you'd know where I was and that you'd be transported right back to Earth to wait for me."

"Well, instead I was stuck in Evadere to figure out a world I knew nothing about, and the only person I could depend upon was Jo, a little Scave girl." She turned around and faced us.

Emry bit his lip as though he had just realized Jo had witnessed our conversation. I could feel Emry's tension and Jo's anxiety to the situation. "Thank you for bringing Anna back to me safely," he finally said. "I apologize you had to hear all of that about your people."

Jo said nothing, just returned to flipping through a book she had found with lots of pictures.

"So what was your plan?" I asked. "Were you going to return to Earth for me?"

"Of course," he said quickly.

"When?"

He ran his fingers through his hair again. "As soon as my training was completed. As soon as I'd figured things out."

"What exactly is entailed in your training?"

He shrugged. "My mother is trying to teach me about my powers, how to use them properly."

"Well, that's a relief." I smiled. "Someone has to."

"Very funny." Emry grinned back. "I want you in my life, Anna James, human or not." "Emry, you're a prince." I put my hands over my face as I felt the tears return.

He wrapped his arms around me and drew me close. I was sure I was getting dirt all over his beautiful clothes. "None of this matters in the scheme of you and I," he whispered. "Nothing comes between us. Do you hear me?"

I wept against his chest. "Nothing," he repeated.

"I don't belong to Evadere," I cried.

"You belong where I am."

Emry and I stood there like that for a few minutes, intertwined together in this twisted world that had gleams of beauty in it once more, now that it was owned by Emry Logan. Surely, if anyone could take the pain out of Evadere, it was him. He would stay at the castle and learn about his powers of royalty, and I would teach him what I knew from the Scaves' standpoint, how things had gotten way out of hand decades before he had ever been born. Together we could figure this out and come up with a solution.

"Can I stay?" I asked him. "I don't have to go back to Earth, do I?"

"I would love for you to stay here at the castle with me. I'm sure my mother won't mind. She's away right now on a trip." He saw my concern. "Trust me?"

I pressed my lips together in a smile and nodded.

He flashed a smile back and then he bent forward to kiss me. It felt like forever since I had felt the magic of his touch. Then I took a few sudden steps backward. "What is it?" he asked.

"Oh, Emry," I said. I must smell so gross. "I'm so disgustingly dirty. I need a shower so bad."

"Oh, that." He sighed, relieved, and extended a hand.

Placing my hand in his, I could see the dirt covering my skin intertwined in his own flawless fingers.

"We'll get you both cleaned up and then food, lots of food. How's that sound?"

"Good." We walked over to the door, Jo following. He opened it, and we stepped out into the broad hallway. It wrapped around the top of the spiral staircase so that you could see below to the ground level.

I tried to enjoy the details of the castle. We made it around one corner of the staircase when something above in the hallway caught my eye. It was a small, middle-aged woman with gray curls tied back away from her face. She was hunched over on the floor of the hallway on hands and knees, scrubbing away, a bucket at her side. She stopped her work for a moment and looked up at me. Our eyes met. I saw loneliness in her eyes, along with terror. She quickly looked away and began fervently cleaning once more.

Chapter 8

"Honestly, Emry, I leave you for one day, and I get news there's a human *and* a Scave living under my roof now ..."

I pushed a strand of hair out of my eyes to see who had just burst into the room. It was an older woman with brown hair pulled neatly back, away from her face. She wore a purple dress decorated in crystals, and I assumed by the crown on her head with matching crystals, that this was Queen Atavia. She huffed and put her hands on her hips.

"A human and a Scave both in your room? What is going on here, Emry?" she asked, struggling to remain calm.

I looked to the opposite side of the table where Jo put down the spoon she had been using for her breakfast. Her eyes were wide in alarm. She looked posed, as though she was ready to run if needed. She was used to escaping confrontation, not being face to face with it. Emry rose to his feet. His hair was still tousled as he hadn't fixed it yet for the day. He kept glancing from his mother to me.

"Mother, this is Anna," he said calmly.

I stood and joined Emry. I didn't know if I should shake the queen's hand or not, but by the look on her face, I decided to keep my distance.

Atavia's eyes widened in disbelief. "Anna? Anna James?"

I nodded my head, slowly. My hands moved to my hair where I tried to comb it quickly with my fingers and toss it behind my back.

"But how … how did you get here?" she asked.

I frowned.

Emry wrapped his arm around my shoulders. "She was left on the beach. No one took her back to Earth. You assured me she was safe."

The beautiful queen looked to the ceiling and took a deep breath. Then she looked back to her son.

"I'm not sure how such a terrible mistake was made. My informants told me she had been returned. I will get to the bottom of it," she said, a little too quickly. "I must say, I'm very surprised to learn that a human made it the entire way here and survived that journey."

My mouth dropped open.

"God was watching over her," Emry said.

Queen Atavia raised an eyebrow. She pressed her lips together. "Why yes, I suppose He was."

"This is Jo." Emry looked over to her. She still looked like a scared mouse. "It's okay, Jo. No one is going to hurt you. You're safe."

Jo crouched lower in her chair, her eyes to the floor.

"She's a Scave?" Atavia asked, her tone threatening again. "As in a Scave that has been with Karn her entire life?"

"Calm down, Mother," Emry pleaded.

"Are you aware that Karn destroyed my family?" she asked Jo accusingly. "He murdered my husband in front of my very eyes and has been hunting my son ever since so that I was unable to raise my own child. He had to live among humans."

I saw Jo's hand begin to tremble. I walked over to her and wrapped my arms around her.

"She put her life on the line to get Anna here," Emry said. "They defiled Karn and even lost one along the way. They've been through a terrible ordeal to get here, their lives at stake all along. Look at her, Mother; she's terrified. I couldn't leave her alone last night. They both slept safe and sound in my bed while I watched over them."

Atavia's face twisted in disgust.

"Her actions outweigh her background," he continued. "If it wasn't for her, Anna wouldn't be here.

She's our friend, our ally."

Atavia rubbed her temples. "This goes against everything within me to allow them to stay."

"Anna is my girlfriend," he snapped. "She's staying. Jo is, too."

I met Atavia's stare. She immediately loathed me and Jo. Something made me think that if the situation had been different, if Emry hadn't been here and I had to have faced Atavia alone, I'd be a goner. I also didn't believe that my being left on the beach was an accident. Atavia obviously hated humans and hated even more the fact that her son was with one. This wasn't in her plan, and so her leaving me behind on Evadere was her scheme to get rid of me. She never in a million years would've thought I would survive both Scaves and contributors to be standing in the castle. Now that

I think back on it, I'm not sure how I escaped all those situations, but as Emry said, God was on my side. There was no other answer for my survival, but now I had a rival on my hands. The queen had been reunited with her beloved son, and I was still in the picture. This interrupted whatever plans she had for him, and she didn't like it. Furthermore, a Scave was in her midst. It was like we had just marched in here and stabbed her in the heart, yet she wasn't comfortable with kicking us out of the castle against Emry's will. She needed her son to stay on her side. I'd have to sleep with one eye open from now on. The pit of my stomach twisted. I could only hope that the love between Emry and I was strong enough to withstand a scheming queen, who I'm sure had powers greater than any I'd seen.

"Very well," Atavia said, her voice empty of all emotion. "They may stay, but I will get their own rooms prepared."

Emry started to protest.

"Is there something I'm unaware of?" She raised her eyebrows at her son. "Are you and Anna *married*?"

Emry glanced at me. "No ..."

"That's what I thought. Then she spends her nights in her own room." With that, Atavia turned on her heels, her purple gown twirling with the movement as she exited the large bedroom.

When it was time for dinner, I anxiously walked over to my mirror in my newly prepared bedroom completely independent from Emry's.

Atavia had many servants, and one had helped me into a dark rose-colored gown. They pulled my hair back for me, leaving a few strands to fall on my back. I hadn't seen Emry or Jo since this morning, and I didn't have anything to do except stay in my room all day and think way too much about the Atavia situation and how much she hated me. I had myself all worked up and worried sick. Someone had just come to my door and announced dinner was being served on the main floor. After giving myself one more look in the mirror, I had decided there was nothing I was going to do to erase the dark circles that still lingered under my eyes or the weight I felt I had lost over the last few days. This was as good as I was going to look tonight, and I better get going downstairs in case I got lost in this gigantic maze of a castle. I wasn't even sure where Emry's room was in relation to mine.

I was one of the last ones coming into dinner. Everyone immediately became quiet and stared at me.

It was as if I had been the topic of conversation all day and probably was, considering I was a human. I felt uncomfortable and clumsy. My gown began to itch.

There was a long rectangular table in the center of the room. Most of the chairs were already filled as I searched face after face, knowing no one. Someone stood. Emry. He smiled warmly at me. I returned the smile with a sigh of relief as he motioned for me to come over to him and sit. He held out my chair.

"You look beautiful," he whispered in my ear as I sat.

"Thank you," I replied, my cheeks flushing red as everyone continued to stare.

One by one, conversation amongst the guests resumed again. I took a deep breath and leaned into Emry, who squeezed my hand as if he understood exactly what I was going through.

"Who are all these people?" I asked.

"Some are my family—uncles, aunts, cousins. Ben is up there at the end," he said, motioning with his head.

I met eyes with Ben, who gave me a little wave.

"Some are contributors from outside the castle, close friends of my mother's. She has different guests every night."

I scanned the faces again. Jo wasn't here. A twinge of worry filled me.

Then the heavy chairs screeched against the cement floor as everyone pushed them out and stood. I quickly fumbled to do the same. With a noisy entrance of thrusting the doors open, in bounded Queen Atavia. She had changed into another gown, this one a brilliant gold color with jewels and gems dangling from her ears and neck. Her nose went in the air as she flashed a grin and hurried over to her seat. She raised her arms and gestured for everyone to sit. She glanced at me momentarily, her eyes becoming dark as she did so, then she quickly looked away and began merrily chatting with the woman on her right-hand side.

"Hungry?" Emry asked.

"Yes." I smiled again at him.

"You okay?" he whispered.

I smoothed my hands over the front of my dress. "Fine, thanks."

He jabbed me teasingly with his elbow. "I know; it's a little overwhelming. You have to admit, though, it's a little exciting at the same time."

Emry looked so happy. He looked like he fit in here with all these handsome people. I had to admit, I was thrilled to be by his side.

"Emry, where's Jo?" I asked, but then the queen started talking, and everyone turned their attention toward her.

Queen Atavia stood. I heard chairs go as a few people scrambled to their feet.

"No, please, sit, relax," she told them. "Raise your glasses with me. Join me in a toast."

Everyone grabbed their glasses. I couldn't believe how heavy it was as I raised it in the air with the rest of them.

"I am such a happy woman. The pieces are fitting together, my friends. My son, my sweet, sweet, Emry is home once again." She smiled adoringly at him. He returned the smile. "He, soon, will be king. So join me, my friends, my family. Let us drink to King Emry. His father would be so very proud of the man he's become."

"To King Emry! To King Emry!" they chanted out after her.

I pressed my lips together and forced a smile. Why didn't I feel right? Shouldn't I be happy that I was here with him in Evadere? I should be happy just to be alive, but something felt off. Perhaps it was just the ill feelings I felt toward Atavia. Maybe it was just because I didn't feel as charming and beautiful as all of these strangers around me. I had no idea what they thought about me, but I could guess. After all, I was merely a human.

Emry stood. Everyone looked to me. "Stand," he said to me.

"Emry, no …" I protested.

He pulled me to my feet. I pressed my lips together and tried to avoid the looks that everyone was giving to me.

"Please welcome my love, Anna James. She's had rough travels to the castle. I'm so grateful she's here." He turned to me and smiled. "She saved my life on Earth."

"To Anna," someone shouted out.

"To Anna," others followed.

"Thank you," I muttered, before sitting back down even more uncomfortable now that I had been so formally introduced.

The food was served. It was some sort of tender meat, potatoes, and vegetables. It was delicious, and I relished every bite, swearing never to take food for granted again after being without it for days in the wilderness of Evadere. What I assumed was some sort of wine in my cup was very sweet as well. It went down smoothly after each bite, and soon I felt a little intoxicated, a little more relaxed and less worried about the situation I had gotten myself into. My thoughts drifted to the fact that Emry Logan was soon to be a king of an entire planet. It was as if the idea of it hadn't truly processed before as it was now. It was amazing, and I was grateful to be a part of his experience. He was going from Lainey Tritt and prison on Earth, to the luxuries of a glorious castle that had everything anyone could ever want. King Emry. I repeated it within my mind. Emry turned and looked at me. I grinned. I wondered if he could tell I was now a bit tipsy. It didn't matter really. I didn't know why I was letting these people make me feel insignificant. Sure, I was human, but who knows, I could be their queen someday, and they'd have to listen to what I had to say, to all of my opinions. Emry loved *me*. Yes, I was sure I'd be queen of Evadere right by his side.

"So, Anna …"

My head shot up as someone was actually trying to make conversation with me. It was an older gentleman who was seated across the table from me. He was balding with a thick black mustache curled slightly on the ends.

"Prince Emry said you had rough travels. You didn't come with him, I presume?" the man asked.

"No," I replied.

"How did you get here then? Do tell." He stabbed a fork full of meat and stuffed it into his mouth.

I realized everyone else was staring at me. I was the center of attention, a position that I always tried to avoid. "Well, I was found by a Scave girl."

"A Scavenger?" a woman asked in alarm.

"Yes," I answered slowly.

"Uh, unhealthy creatures," someone else stated. "I can only image all the diseases you were exposed to."

I lowered my eyebrows at their comments. "She was ... fine; actually really nice."

"How did you get food?" the man across the table asked. "Don't Scaves steal their food?"

I wasn't sure how to answer. I felt trapped by the question. "Um ..."

"Why don't you get to the good parts?" someone else encouraged. "Were you ever in danger?"

"I was chased by a group of contributors. I got stoned in the back," I said flatly.

Emry glared at me. "What? You didn't mention that to me."

"So much happened," I stuttered.

Atavia looked thoroughly amused that I had been in pain. She would've been even more amused if I

had died. That I was sure of.

"They mistook you for a Scave," a younger man said. "Us contributors only stone Scaves."

"Well, she's human," a woman stated.

"True," he agreed. "Basically the same thing."

I narrowed my eyes at them. Did Atavia bring these people here to belittle me, or was it everyone's nature here on Evadere to stereotype people?

The man across the table dabbed his mouth with a napkin. "Ms. James, you didn't happen to meet the infamous Scave Karn, did you?"

"Surely not," someone said.

I nervously took another sip of my drink and set it back down. "Yes, I did."

"What?" a woman hissed out in shock. "What did he look like? Is he as gruesome as they say?"

I nodded at her. "He's horrific, like a beast."

"He didn't slay you?"

"Obviously not. She's sitting over there, isn't she?" Someone snickered.

"He tried," I whispered. "A Scave boy spared my life, but he was killed by contributors, too."

"He probably tried to steal," someone suggested.

"Only to try to get caught, so we would get captured by royalty," I told them.

"Sounds like a foolish plan to me."

"Me, too."

I looked up at Atavia, who was savoring every moment of my discomfort. She had her elbows propped up on the table as she crossed her heavily jeweled fingers. My temper flared.

"How dare you judge the Scaves?" I felt my voice grow louder, the alcohol making me bolder with every sip. "They were cast away. They have nothing. How else could they live other than to steal?

They have no other means of survival."

"They weren't meant to live," a woman commented.

I glared at her. "Who are you to decide?" I yelled out. "What makes them so different than you?" "Well, of course, my dear, they have no powers," the man across the table stated with a smirk. "Neither do I," I said.

"Well ..." he hesitated. I could tell he was about to say something against me, but he changed his mind after glancing Emry's way.

"I feel sorry for the Scaves," I continued. "They're a horrific people because of the way they've been forced to live. How can you blame them for having ill feelings toward contributors?"

"My dear, Anna." Atavia spoke for the first time in this conversation. "You don't know what you're saying. You only know one side of the story."

"I lived that side of the story for a few days. It was terrible." "The Scaves are out to kill us," she said calmly. "They want Emry dead. Is that what you want?"

"Of course not," I snapped. I had suddenly lost my appetite. This dinner had been a trap. I glanced at Emry. Why wasn't he saying anything? Shouldn't he be defending me? "This world needs peace."

"Peace," Atavia said. "That's something we all desire. That's what we've always strived to create."

"By labeling powerless babies as Scaves and casting them away for dead?" "Anna," Emry said in a scolding tone.

I narrowed my eyes at him then. I had offended his guests, his mother.

"Yes, we are trying to eat," Atavia added. "Ms. James is obviously still sleep deprived."

"No ..." I started to say, but Emry put his hand on my knee, stopping me. I sat back in my chair, discouraged. No one would listen to me. No one cared about my opinions. Not even him. I was outnumbered. My sudden burst of boldness vanished.

"Your majesty." A servant girl came in through another door. She approached Atavia and whispered something in her ear.

Atavia clasped her hands in delight. "She made it. I'm so thrilled. Please make sure she gets food served immediately, and send her right in."

I watched the servant girl leave and seconds later burst back through the door with a tall, thin woman at her side. She brought her over to Atavia, who then stood and placed her hand approvingly on the woman's back.

"Friends," Atavia announced. "Please welcome a daughter of a dear friend of mine, Raleigh." She turned to her. "Raleigh, you can sit … over there." She pointed. "There's an empty chair right next to my son, Prince Emry." Atavia looked at me and smirked.

Raleigh strode over to us in a dark wispy dress that flowed behind her as she moved. She had long, shiny blonde hair that reached the middle of her back, curled at the ends. Her face was pale, and her lips had been painted a deep red color. Her cheeks were rosy, and her eyes painted back with long, curly lashes. Emry stood and pulled out a chair for her right next to him. I hated her immediately.

"Prince Emry, it's so very nice to finally meet you," Raleigh said, batting her long lashes at him. "Likewise," he replied, kindly.

The servants rushed in with food for Raleigh and piled it on her plate.

"Oh, my," she said, smiling. "I couldn't possibly eat this much." She giggled and looked at Emry once again.

The man across the table who had badgered me, spoke up. "Ms. Raleigh, what a delight for you to join us. What group are you from?"

The woman hadn't touched her food yet. She unfolded a napkin and spread it out on her lap.

"Clothes."

"Really?" he said.

She nodded, her flawless hair falling in blonde tendrils around her face.

"She's adding fashion to her clothes. She's more like a designer," Atavia told him. "Don't be shy, Raleigh. Tell them your ideas."

She smiled, loving every minute of the attention. "Well, I just think we need to add a little more fashion to our clothes, have more choices. We've had the same designs for such a long time. Although the gowns and pant suits are beautiful, it wouldn't hurt to have them updated a little."

"What a wonderful idea," a woman said.

"I would love for that to happen," another agreed.

"It's in the works," Atavia told them.

Raleigh took a sip of her drink and daintily set it back down. "After all, even the humans live in world of fashion."

Everyone's eyes flashed to me instantly.

"Is that true, Ms. James?" the man asked.

I glared at him but didn't answer. I was ready to go. They obviously already had all of their minds made up about me.

"Would you excuse me?" I said, standing. "I'm not feeling well suddenly. I think I'm going to go back to my room."

"Are you okay?" Emry asked.

I nodded. "Will you come with me?"

"Actually," Atavia interrupted. "Emry, I was hoping you could show Raleigh around the castle.

She's never had a tour before, and she'd love to see the place. Wouldn't you, Raleigh?"

"Oh, yes, very much," Raleigh replied.

Emry stood. "It wouldn't be polite to ignore a guest." He turned to me. "I promise I'll come check on you in a little while, okay?" he whispered in my ear.

I looked at Raleigh, then Atavia, then him. "Do whatever you have to do."

He kissed me on the forehead and sat back down in his chair.

I stared for a few seconds, shocked that he was staying and I was going. I hurried out of the room and headed straight for the staircase. I sat down on one of the steps and buried my face in my arms resting on my knees.

Things had changed in the blink of an eye. Emry had finally found his place. Of course he was a prince, why wouldn't he be? Nobody wanted him to be with a *human*, but I wasn't about to give up. I had tried letting go of Emry Logan before, and vowed never to do it again. We both needed time to adjust to this new lifestyle. He needed a little bit of space, and no matter how angry that made me, I was just going to have to accept it.

I sat up and crossed my arms. Raleigh. The thought of her made me burn with more fury. It was as though Atavia had purposely brought her here to compete with me, and Raleigh was beautiful and elegant, all the things I felt far from being. The jealousy feeling was reminiscent of what I had felt when knowing Emry had been married to Candy on Earth. I hated the helpless feeling that went along with it this time. Emry and Raleigh would be alone together tonight as he showed her around the castle. I could just picture her now, laughing and flipping her silky blonde hair behind her back.

I needed to get up and go somewhere to cool off. If I stayed here, I'd only see Emry and Raleigh together, and then who knows what I'd do. I might go off the deep end and do something or say something I would regret. I had to trust him, give him some space. Atavia, Raleigh ... they couldn't come between us.

I moved away from the stairs and roamed around the main floor. I tried to distract myself by paying special attention to the artsy detail that covered every inch of this place. Then I walked through a narrow corridor and a strange door caught my eye at the end of it. Then I recognized it. It led down to the dungeon. Jo entered my mind. Surely she wasn't down there again. She hadn't been at dinner.

Atavia seemed perfectly capable of locking Jo back up behind Emry's back. I wouldn't put it past her. Something told me she was down there.

I had to pull back very hard just to get the door to budge as it was extremely heavy. I looked backward to make sure no one was watching when I heard the screechy noise it made as I pulled it open wider so I could fit through. Seeing no one, I closed the door behind me as I made my way down the dark staircase. I could feel the dampness increase with each step. There was a small torch lit along the wall. This place reminded me of something I would've seen in a movie. It was creepy, cold, and full of shadows. It was different being here for the second time. This time, I was all alone. My breathing became shallow as I grabbed the torch and held it out in front of me.

Atavia didn't hold many prisoners, and from what I could tell of the small dungeon, they didn't stay here long. I wondered how the whole judicial system worked here. Was there a counsel, or did Atavia just have say over everyone?

I held the torch out. It was so quiet, I could hear my own heart beating away in my chest.

"Jo?" I whispered. I cleared my throat. "Jo?" I said a little louder. There was no response.

You shouldn't be down here, I scolded myself. I held the torch up to the first cell on my left. It was empty. I took a few more steps and held it out to the right. Again, empty. My feet clumsily shuffled along.

"Jo?" I called out. "Anyone?"

Moving to the next set of cells, these were the last ones. I saw a wall up ahead, indicating this was all that was down here. I held the torch up to the right again. A face peered at me pressed up against the bars. I screamed and jumped back. An eerie cackle escaped from the prisoner's mouth. I took a deep breath in an attempt to compose myself.

I moved closer, realizing I was safe on the other side of the bars, but still feeling the panic zipping within me. I held the light up and squinted my eyes for a moment, trying to focus on the face. What I saw made me gasp and jump back. No, this couldn't be true. I covered my mouth. It wasn't Jo, but it was someone I knew … someone I thought I'd never have to see again.

Chapter 9

"What are you doing here?" she growled at me.

I couldn't see her face anymore as I was standing back, but the glimpse of her face I'd had a moment ago was haunting.

"Me?" I said. "What are *you* doing here? I thought you were exiled to Earth." I stepped forward.

The light illuminated upon Mrs. Anderson's face.

"How did you know that?" she snapped.

The voice didn't match the face. She seemed freaked out here, the complete opposite of how composed she had been while on Earth. I had never heard her raise her voice once. I remember it had driven me crazy that she could almost yell with a controlled voice, but now, her emotions were no longer bound.

"How dare you be here?" she continued. "You think you're so clever, don't you?"

I stared as the torch light reflected in Mrs. Anderson's pupils, tiny flames dancing in her wicked eyes.

"I'm dumbfounded Atavia even permits you here. Do you know what she thinks of humans? It's all your fault that I'm here."

"My fault?" I raised my eyebrows.

"This is all about him."

"Who?"

"Don't play stupid with me. You know that I mean Emry Logan. You've done nothing but ruin my plans to get rid of him once and for all. He's no good. You have no idea what you're messing with."

Mrs. Anderson narrowed her eyes. "I can't believe I'm looking at you here, of all places."

I felt a lump begin to form in my throat. "I don't understand what you have against him. He's a good person."

She chuckled. "Humans know nothing about powers, because they have none. Here, everything is about power. Everything is controlled by it. Everyone only strives for more. Emry is Atavia's child.

Atavia is pure evil."

"She loves Emry."

"She loves power more. I was trying to get rid of him before he matured into his powers, while he was still clueless of his heritage on Earth, but of course, you had to stick your nose into all of that. Please, enlighten me, Ms. James. How has your beloved Emry been since he's been here? Has he been as attentive to your every need?" she asked.

I remained silent, biting the inside of my lip so that Mrs. Anderson wouldn't know she had struck a nerve.

She grinned and pressed her face even further against the bars. "Because he's power hungry, too.

They become obsessed with it. It takes over and controls even the deepest of emotions, even *love*." She hesitated for a moment. "Atavia doesn't view Emry as her son. He's merely another product for her to control, to use at her will to do what she wants. The entire royal bloodline needs to be destroyed." Mrs. Anderson's hands released their tight grasp on the bars and fell to her sides. "The task would be completed if you hadn't interfered. I had him right where I wanted him."

"You don't know what you're saying." I tried to sound harsh, but my voice came out as timid.

"No, *you* don't know what you're saying. You know nothing about these matters. You're merely human, and you're blinded by love; a love that doesn't even exist between you and Emry Logan." She cackled again. "You'll find out soon enough. One thing you'd better get through your head fast, Ms. James. You're powerless in a world of power."

"What's going on here?" a voice shouted out.

I turned around to see the silhouette of a figure headed straight toward me. It was Jillianne, Atavia's right hand woman. Her eyebrows were lowered as she tromped toward me with her own torch.

"You're not permitted down here," she shrieked in her annoying, high-pitched voice. She glanced at Mrs. Anderson and then grabbed my wrist and spun me around.

"Hey!" I yelled. "What do you think you're doing?"

Jillianne continued to sink her nails into my skin, forcing me to leave the dungeon. "I'm taking you straight to the queen to inform her of what you've done."

"What I've done?" I asked, my legs clumsily following the short, pudgy woman as I tried not to trip over her.

"Oh, the *queen*," Mrs. Anderson hissed. "Do tell her I said hello."

Once on the main floor, Jillianne shut the door to the dungeon and clamped onto my arm again.

"Stop," I said. "That hurts. I'm coming."

She glared at me and pointed to a door on the side of the corridor. "There. Go."

The room was very bare with a lush rug in the center and a small desk in the corner. Large windows from the floor to the ceiling were blocked out by wooden shutters.

"Wait here," Jillianne instructed me. "And if you move..."

"What exactly are you threatening?" I asked, walking into the center of the room. Jillianne huffed, turned on her heels and left the room.

I stared at the open door. Should I stay here? I was in trouble, but for what exactly? What was Atavia going to accuse me of? I rubbed my forehead and shut my eyes for a few seconds. Seeing Mrs. Anderson felt uncomfortably similar to what I had gone through when Emry was in prison. Instead of our bad luck ending on Earth, it had followed us to Evadere where again we were faced with a whole new group of people who didn't want Emry and I to be together. I felt the frustration overwhelm me. I had to remain calm. I had to think things through. I didn't know what I was up against. Everything was brand new. I couldn't let them make me be out to be the bad guy. I took a deep breath and opened my eyes right in time to see Atavia and Ben Hanley rushing into the room, Jillianne trailing behind.

"What is the explanation for all of this?" Atavia asked.

"Tell her," Jillianne said, her squeaky voice only increasing my agitation. "Go on," she insisted.

"Tell the queen what you were doing."

I stared at them for a moment. Ben wasn't looking at me directly. He was running his fingers along a piece of artwork on the wall. He was either distracted or bored. I couldn't make up my mind which one.

"I was in the dungeon," I said.

"Yes, yes she was." Jillianne put her hands on her wide hips.

"Why were you there?" Atavia asked.

I sighed.

"Listen, I have guests to tend to," Atavia began.

"By all means, please go back to what you were doing," I said. "Tend to your guests."

She narrowed her eyes at me. I saw a muscle on the side of her face twinge as she clenched her teeth together. "I knew you were going to be a pest."

"Excuse me?" I snapped, shocked she was being so forward.

"Let me be perfectly blunt. I don't like you."

"Well, that's obvious," I said. "Because I'm a human."

"Among other reasons," she snapped. "You're distracting my Emry."

"*Your* Emry?"

She ignored me. "Why were you conversing with the prisoner?"

"Mrs. Anderson?"

"Witch Hanley," Jillianne corrected me.

I glanced Ben's way. He looked at me out of the corner of his eye. "I didn't even know she was down there," I blurted out. "I was looking for Jo."

"Jo?" Atavia asked, raising her eyebrows.

Anger zipped through me. She hadn't even taken the time to know her name. "Yeah, you know, the Scave I brought along with me."

Atavia and Jillianne glanced at each other, confusion on their faces.

"Why would she be down there? You know Emry released her at your request." Atavia glared at me. She couldn't stand the fact that Emry had an ounce of affection toward me.

"I just assumed that's where she was."

"She has a room upstairs, like you. I convinced her not to come to dinner," Atavia confessed. "Why did you do that?" I asked.

"This is *my* castle." Her eyes grew dark in fury. "I do not have to *ever* explain myself to you."

"Can barely stomach a human at the dinner table, let alone a human and a Scave," Jillianne mumbled.

"If it wasn't for Emry," Atavia said. "You'd be in that dungeon right alongside Witch Hanley."

I frowned. "There's no surprise there, Atavia."

"Queen Atavia!" Jillianne bellowed out.

I took a deep breath. "Can I go to my room now?"

Atavia folded her hands in front of her as she made an attempt not to flip out on me. "We need to have a little chat about the prisoner."

"Why is she back here, anyway?" I asked.

"The less you know..." Atavia began, but Ben butted in.

"She's my sister, Anna." Ben turned toward me in a gentle voice. He wore tan pants and a matching shirt that made him seem less tense as I had only seen him in suits. "We have the same parents. That's the only link. She's a monster. She has done nothing but stir up Emry's life. You saw what she did on Earth."

"Where she was exiled…" I said.

He nodded. "You see, she and I are from the protector contributors. There aren't many of us, but we have powers to protect royalty. She decided to use her powers to try black magic and all kinds of things she shouldn't have gotten into. She was warned, and still she pursued works of evil and the death of royalty."

"Why does she want to hurt Emry?" I asked, trusting him more than the other two.

He spun around and turned his back to me. "She's just not right, mentally. You know how people on Earth can become mentally sick?"

"Yeah..."

"Well, that's how people here can become as well. She's not right in the head. She is impulsive and at times, very out of control. She couldn't be trusted, not here, so she was exiled to Earth. But then, somehow she found Emry there, too. I'm Emry's protector, and my very own sister was creating havoc."

"If you must know," Atavia continued. "I decided Witch Hanley can't be trusted no matter where she is. She just won't give up. She's so fixated on destroying Emry. We brought her back and she's now... under investigation."

"What does that mean exactly, under investigation?" I asked.

"I'm going back to the dining hall," Atavia said, ignoring my question. She pointed at me with her jeweled finger. "Stay out of the dungeon. Stay out of my way," she warned.

I watched her and Jillianne leave. Ben lingered in the room momentarily.

"I'm sure it's a lot to take in, all of this," he waved his arm, "Emry, the way things are," he said quietly.

I took a deep breath. "What's going to happen to Mrs. Anderson?"

"I don't know yet..."

"Ben, she's your sister. Isn't there some part of you that wants to help her if she does have problems with her mind?"

"Like I said, Anna, we just have the same parents; that's all. Do you want her to keep going after Emry?" he asked.

"Of course not," I answered. "I just don't get it."

"There's going to be a lot you don't get," he told me. "You're going to have to learn to just let it be." He headed toward the door. "A maidservant will be in to show you back to your room. Enjoy the rest of your evening." With that, he was gone, leaving me alone with my thoughts.

A few moments later, a woman entered the room. She had been the one I had seen upstairs scrubbing the floor. She had a look of terror on her face as our eyes met again, hers dark and weary.

She looked to the floor as she stopped and stood in front of me.

"Are you the one supposed to *escort* me back to my room?" I asked, frowning.

She nodded.

I stared at her meek appearance. Who was she? Were there contributors made just to be servants of royalty? "Do you speak?" I asked her.

She shook her head quickly, no.

A mute? Surely not. Wouldn't that be considered a defect ... unless she still had powers? This woman provoked my interest. Out of the corner of my eye, I saw a flash of blonde hair pass by the room, followed by a flirtatious laugh. Raleigh. She was probably on her little tour with Emry right now. After the evening I had just had, I knew I couldn't stomach seeing them together. I needed to go back to my room and try to sleep off this horrible day.

"Okay. I'll follow you," I said, submitting to Atavia's wishes.

The strange woman spun around and hurried out of the room. I took a deep breath and trailed behind her as she led me to the spiral staircase. We walked up the steps in silence, neither Raleigh, nor Emry fortunately in sight.

We made it to the top of the staircase when the woman rounded a corner instead of going straight. I didn't remember this corner. This wasn't the way to my room. I hesitated, watching the woman disappear. Uneasiness filled me as I wasn't sure what to do. Then I saw her black beady eyes peer around the corner at me. She quickly grabbed my arm and pulled me toward her.

"What is it?" I asked.

She looked around for a moment and then pulled me into a dark, small room full of cleaning supplies. She glanced out in the hallway one more time before shutting the door.

"Why do you look so scared?"

She looked to the floor and then up into my eyes. "Are you a human?" she whispered.

My eyes widened at her words. "I thought you couldn't talk," I hissed.

She grabbed my arm harder this time and pulled me close. "Please, I need to know."

I narrowed my eyes at her and jerked my arm back. "Yes, I am. I thought everyone already knew that."

"I wanted to make sure. I've never seen a human before."

"Well, here I am," I said, all kinds of questions forming in my head about this strange woman.

"How did you get here?"

"Emry transported me..."

"No," she interrupted. "I mean, how'd you get to the castle?"

"Oh." I crossed my arms. "I'm lucky I got here alive. That world out there is a brutal one."

"Yes," she agreed. "It is."

I stared at her for a few seconds. "Why are you called the queen's maidservant? Are there contributors that serve royalty?"

She swallowed and began playing with her fingers. "I have something I want to tell you, but I'm not sure if I should."

My pulse began to race.

"I don't know if I can trust you or not," she added.

"Why wouldn't you be able to?" I asked.

She examined my face. "Because you're with Emry, and he's *her* son. She'd kill me if she knew."

"Atavia?"

She nodded.

"I promise you can trust me," I said gently, trying to ease the information out of her.

She licked her lips and then flattened a stray gray curl back with her palm that had fallen into her face. "I'm a human, too."

I gasped. "What?"

Fear filled her eyes once again as her secret had just been revealed. "Please," she begged. "You can't tell anyone."

"I won't. I won't. How did *you* get here? How long have you been here?"

She nodded, realizing I was full of questions. "It took me a long, long time to figure out how I got here. For awhile, it was as if I just appeared here. It even took me some time to figure out this wasn't Earth. It happened when I was young. I got hungry and wandered in a contributor group's place of living. I got captured and taken here. Atavia thinks I'm a Scave."

"Wow," I muttered, considering what she was saying. "She thinks you're a Scave, and she lets you live here?"

"Yes," the woman continued. "Only because she saw how well kept I was. She assumes that contributors had taken care of me for years before being found out and that's why I had such nice looking teeth, hair, and clothes. I was too afraid as a girl to speak, and I didn't understand what was happening, so the queen has always assumed I'm not able to speak at all. I think if it wasn't for my appearance, she'd have killed me."

"So all this time you've been her servant?"

"Yeah, I clean the castle in exchange for a nice room and food," she replied.

"So someone from royalty had to have transported you here," I said, thinking about how terrible her life must be, catering to Atavia.

She nodded. "Your name is Anna James?"

"Yeah."

She gave a little smile and held out her hand. "I'm Cassie Banesberry."

I extended my arm to shake her hand, but my knees felt weak. I wasn't sure if I was going to pass out or not. My hands reached backward, feeling for where the wall was so I could lean on it.

"Are you okay?" she asked, rushing to my side and helping to prop me up.

"Your name," I managed to say. "You said Cassie Banesberry."

Her eyebrows lowered. "They don't know my name here. Like I said, I've never spoken..."

I shook my head as I was still depending on the wall for support. "No, no. You don't understand," I told her. "I know who you are."

"What?" She took a few steps backward. "How is that possible?"

I stared at the woman with her gray hair and remembered her as a little girl in the abandoned Banesberry house, a dusty picture of her and Lucas. "This is just amazing really. I met your family while doing research on Lucas. I know all about how they adopted him into the family after finding him. I even know that you disappeared after Lucas became angry. That must be when he transported you here."

"By accident," Cassie said. "It took me awhile to figure it all out. I had to piece bits of information I overhead through people here to understand what happened."

I felt a little better and attempted standing once more successfully. "So Lucas Banesberry must've been royalty, and he must've been hiding from the Scaves, too, on Earth?"

She nodded. "He is a cousin of Emry's. I've heard them speak of him. Like Emry, he didn't know who he was, though; didn't understand his powers." She paused for a moment, her face becoming tense. "Lucas was my very best friend, and my brother. No one understood him like I did. I thought after I'd figured it all out, that he had transported me here, that someday he'd come back to find me, but he's never come. And now

Emry's here. Lucas would be older, like me, by now. Why hasn't he come?"

Tears filled my eyes as I could almost feel the pain Cassie had pinned up inside her all these years.

I wondered how long it had taken her to figure out where she was, how she had gotten to Evadere. I wondered how long she'd been waiting for Lucas Banesberry to return and to take her back home. It was so sad.

"He's dead, isn't he?" she whispered.

I wiped a stray tear away from my cheek with the back of my hand. "He was locked away for awhile for being … you know, different. The day he was released, someone shot him. I'm so sorry you had to find out like this." I stepped closer to the woman and hugged her. She wasn't sure what to do, a hug being so very foreign to her as I was certain all affection was. Slowly, she wrapped her arms around my back and hugged me back.

After a few moments, Cassie stepped back, wiping her own tears away. "Thank you for telling me, Anna. I feel so sad that those things had to happen to him. They never spoke of him dying here, but I am relieved to know that he hadn't come just because he had forgotten about me."

"I'm sure he thought about you every day, Cassie."

She pressed her lips together and forced a smile. "Did you see my parents? How are they?"

"I honestly think they didn't do so well after you disappeared. It was hard on them not knowing what happened to you. I only saw your mother."

"She's pretty old now," Cassie said.

I nodded. "She had been sleeping that day. I didn't stay long. Like I said, I was just getting information on Lucas."

"Atavia is mean," Cassie whispered. She glanced around as if there were eyes on the walls. "She has plans for Emry to be king, her kind of king, one that she can control. Don't let her push you around, because she's going to try."

"She's already trying," I told her. "Cassie Banesberry." I shook my head in amazement. It was like I had found a piece to a very large, confusing puzzle. "Wow."

"So glad to have met another human being."

"I can't even imagine what you've gone through." Cassie huffed as if it were too awful to say aloud.

"I'm not sure how, but I'll figure out a way to take you back home," I promised.

Cassie's eyes lit up. "Really?"

I chuckled. "You don't think I'd leave you here, do you?" She shrugged, eyeing me up again.

"I'm not Queen Atavia. I do have a heart." I laughed, and Cassie laughed a little, too.

"Like I said, I'll have to figure it out. We can't expose your secret, that's for sure."

"She'd kill me if she found out I've lied all these years." Cassie paused for a moment, listening.

"It's time we got you back to your room," she said, hurrying to the door of the room and peering out in the hallway. "Please, come quickly."

I rushed out of the little storage unit and saw the tail of Cassie Banesberry's dress whip around the corner as she hurried toward my room.

Chapter 10

I stepped out of the shower and wrapped a towel around myself. I felt refreshed. Even with a million things on my mind, I had managed to sleep very well last night. Emry hadn't come to check on me, though. Raleigh's beautiful face pounced in my mind. I frowned, then immediately tried to erase her face from my thoughts. I wasn't going to allow jealousy to ruin my semi-good mood for the day.

There was a knock on my door. "Yes?" I asked.

"Ms. James, dinner will be served in approximately an hour," someone announced. "Thank you!" I shouted, looking around the room for my clothes.

Dinner was a smaller group this time. I entered the room with my hair still damp but feeling as if all the sleep I had gotten dissolved the circles from underneath my eyes. I was famished, and grinned as Emry hurried to greet me at the door. We embraced momentarily and he gave me a little peck on the cheek.

"Feeling better?" he asked.

I felt the sting return of knowing he hadn't come to check on me. "Yes, actually."

As if reading my mind, he added, "Mother suggested I let you rest today."

"Oh?" I raised my eyebrows and glanced toward Atavia sitting at the table. "That was ... nice of her."

"I have so much to tell you about my powers and what I've been learning." He grinned like a little kid, and just like that, all of the tension melted away from my body.

"Can't wait to hear about it." I weaved my arm inside of his as he escorted me over to the table.

"You look beautiful, by the way," he whispered into my ear.

As we approached the table, Emry led me to an empty chair and held it out for me. There were two men on either side of me. I turned to give him a look.

"And you're sitting where?" I asked.

He turned and looked toward his chair. Raleigh met my glance from behind her silky blonde hair that was covering one of her eyes. "I'm sorry," he mumbled. "Mother put me next to Raleigh."

I felt my ears grow warm in heat.

"It's just because she doesn't know anyone, and mother doesn't want her to feel left out," he quickly explained.

"Oh, and I know everyone?" I asked, sitting down and allowing Emry to push in my chair. I didn't want to look up at Atavia as I could already feel her eyes on me, and I was sure I'd lose my temper if I saw a smirk crossing her lips.

I picked up the cup in front of me and stared at the red liquid inside. Atavia was probably planning on poisoning me, I thought. It'd be smart not to eat or drink anything in this castle. Frowning, I glanced up and realized a man across the table was staring at me. He looked very similar to Emry with the same tan skin, brown hair, only shorter, with blue eyes. I felt color rush into my cheeks and looked up the table at Raleigh and Emry, who seemed to be deep in conversation with each other. Trying to push the jealousy aside, the realization hit me that Jo wasn't here again. I really needed to see her, to make sure she was okay.

"Oh, good!" Atavia exclaimed. "I'm starved."

In floated the servants, their hands carrying platters piled high with food. Among them was Cassie Banesberry. I watched her, but she never glanced my way. A plate of food was placed in front of me, the smell of the meat drifting into my nostrils making my stomach churn in anticipation. A few more plates were set down. I looked up and straight into the face of Jo, who met my eyes. Distracted, she bumped over a cup and spilled the sweet red wine all over the turquoise tablecloth, the liquid extending into the lap of one of Atavia's guests.

"Stupid Scave!" The man jumped to his feet, throwing his arms up in the air, his pants drenched in wine.

Jo retreated against the wall in alarm. It had all happened so fast, it took me a moment to realize that she had been delivering food to the table.

"What did you call her?" I hissed, now rising to my feet.

The man glared at me. "I said, *stupid Scave.* Look at me now. This will never come out."

"It was an accident," I yelled at him, all of my built-up anger exploding from within. "I'm sure you have hundreds of other clothes *exactly* like that."

"My queen, this is an outrage," he shouted.

Atavia sighed. "Get him a cloth, and get this mess cleaned up." She looked Jo's way, who seemed to still be attempting to sink into the wall. "Now!" Atavia yelled.

Jo jumped at the sternness of the queen's voice and hurried out the door.

"Unbelievable," I said aloud. "I thought you were going to take care of Jo, not turn her into one of your futile servants."

"I think it's time you sit down," Emry suggested, his jaw line showing signs of irritation.

My mouth dropped open. "Emry?" I said, the hurt coming on thick. "You agree with what your mother's doing?"

"What's she doing?" he asked.

"Yes, Ms. James, enlighten us," Atavia added.

Jo entered the room and practically threw the cloth at the wine soaked man. She began frantically dabbing at the mess on the table.

"She's turning the girl who saved my life, who got me the entire way here, into a slave. Do I really have to spell it out for you?" My body felt alive with roaring hatred, aimed at the conniving queen.

"Anna, there are things you just don't understand," he said, his tone on the verge of belittlement.

"You're taking her side?" He was now embarrassing me in front of all these people, servants and guests alike.

He took a sip of his own wine and stood. "There's no side to take. Come on, sit now. Let's enjoy our meal."

"I refuse to be in this room for another moment," I cried out, the tears now stinging my eyes and trailing down my cheeks, adding to my public misery. "It seems to me there are things that *you* don't understand, Emry."

"Be careful how you speak to the future king," Atavia warned.

I narrowed my eyes at her. "Emry Logan is not *my* king." The guests gasped.

"I'm a human, remember?"

"Anna," Jo said, hurrying to my side. "It's okay, really."

"How is it okay, Jo?" I asked her. "You at least had your free will before. Now you're bringing them their food? Must I remind you of your heritage, how you were hunted by these exact same people?"

"Anna..." Emry said, coming to my side and taking hold of my wrist.

"Don't," I said, jerking my arm free.

Jo put her hand on my shoulder. "Listen, I know this looks bad in your eyes, but it's not, I swear."

I looked into her calm eyes, my lip trembling.

"I have food in my belly now. I have a warm, comfy place to sleep. I don't fear for my life," she explained.

"You're fine with all of this?"

"Yes, really, I am," she assured me.

I took a deep breath and exhaled loudly. Not even the victim was going to confess to being victimized. I looked like a total idiot.

"My life is better here, now," she said.

"You see?" Atavia said from behind me. "It was your little friend's choice to work for me. She can see what's best for herself, yet you can't. You always yell out persecution."

"The Scaves are persecuted," I growled.

Atavia laughed. Her guests chuckled along with her. "How many times must I remind you? This isn't Earth."

"Please forgive her," Emry said. "She's a human."

"What?" I couldn't believe he had just referred to me as a human in the same manner and tone as everyone else on Evadere had. He had grown up as a human, too. His newly found position in life was going to his head. He was turning into his mother. "Did you really just say that?"

"Anna ..." he said.

I darted around him and straight out the door. I had to get away from all of this. My head was spinning, my emotions intertwining with each other making me feel utterly unstable. I wouldn't stand for how Emry was treating me, for how everyone in there thought of me. There's no way I could put myself through the humiliation of staying in that painful atmosphere, knowing

Raleigh and Atavia were by Emry's side brainwashing him every step of the way, knowing that Jo was going to keep popping in and out of the room serving food to her archenemy.

I turned to the right and sprinted down a hallway I had never been in before. Large double doors were at the end of the hall. I pushed against them with my body to get them to budge. Right outside was some sort of outdoor entertainment area. There were lush plants everywhere. I looked up at the red sky, white stars twinkling down at me. I slumped down onto a bench and put my face in my hands and began to sob, letting everything out.

"Hey!"

I glanced up, and though my tears were blurring my field of vision, I saw a flash of Emry coming toward me. I buried my face in my arms again. Now he was coming to apologize while no one was around. It had hurt before to be away from him, but now it was beginning to hurt even more when around him.

"Do you mind if I sit?"

The voice wasn't Emry's. I sniffed and looked back up. It was the man I had noticed seated at the dinner table. His resemblance to Emry was astonishing. He smiled and sat down next to me on a gray bench, the trickling sound of a running fountain behind us. His blue eyes gleamed underneath the sparkling white stars overhead. I realized I was staring, comparing him to Emry, and quickly looked away.

"I'm Treyu," he said softly.

I wiped my face with the back of my hand and forced the tears to halt in front of this imitation Emry.

"Anna."

He quietly chuckled. "Yes, of course. I know who you are."

"Are you a friend of the queen's?"

"She's my aunt."

"Aunt?"

He grinned, his smile not nearly as stunning as Emry's but welcoming nevertheless. He crossed his arms in front of him and peered up into the sky. "Emry's my cousin. Some say we look alike." He peeked at me out of the corner of his eye.

"Ha," I said. "That's an understatement."

"You think so?" Treyu grinned and jabbed me with his elbow.

"I think you two look very much alike," I stated, realizing I might be giving him the wrong impression by saying so.

"You're upset, that much is obvious. I hated to see you run away like that. After all, I was so very excited to have dinner with a human," Treyu admitted.

I sighed. "It's like I'm a freak show. I should start charging admission."

He laughed. "You're funny, Anna James. I like that." He stared back at me for a moment.

I immediately felt comfortable with him. He was royalty, yet wasn't treating me like an outcast. He had left dinner to come talk to me. "Thanks for coming to check on me. You didn't have to leave for me."

"Oh, nonsense," Treyu said, wrapping an arm around my neck, the smell of his skin intoxicating.

"I'd never met my cousin before, but he's certainly a chip off the old block, so to speak."

"Oh, I hope not." My shoulder slumped under the weight of his arm.

"My aunt can be impossible. Actually, she's always impossible, but Emry... you can tell that even being raised on Earth hasn't changed the fact that he's Calan and Atavia's child," Treyu said.

"Perhaps you thought he was someone else?"

"I don't know." I took a deep breath, and my stomach twisted from being so upset. "He was so kind and gentle. He always consulted with me on everything. I was his biggest supporter, and vice versa."

"Really?" Treyu raised his voice, as if shocked by my explanation of who Emry was. "I don't see any of those things, honestly. Not to burst your bubble or anything. Perhaps you were blinded by love." He stared at me for a moment, assessing what he thought I might be thinking. "Atavia, Emry, they're all about the power."

"I'm so sick of hearing about powers." I sat forward to lean against my knees. Treyu retracted his arm from around me.

"I'm sure you are. You went from a world without it to a world that thrives on it. And Emry, he's been bound up on Earth all this time. Now he knows who he really is. It's only natural he'd want to be trained in the way of his powers, but it's not fair to you who he claims he loves. It's not fair to leave you in the dark on the subject of how this world works." Treyu's eyes moved toward the doors that led back inside. "I don't see what you see in him, honestly."

"But it's Emry," I blurted out, then sighed.

He shrugged. "He's destined to be king. There's enough in that statement to let you know who he really is."

"I know who he really is. He's just..."

"Forgotten? Changed? Conformed into his heritage?" He sighed. "I'm sorry. I'm being harsh, aren't I?"

I pressed my lips together. "No more harsh than anyone else here has treated me. You're the first to sit down and have a conversation with me."

"Have you and Emry spent any time alone together?" Treyu asked.

"No."

"He hasn't shown you around outside?" Treyu sounded surprised again.

"No," I repeated, shrinking farther into my misery.

"Some boyfriend he is."

I looked at Treyu. I couldn't understand his intentions. Was this his way of trying to befriend me, to see where my head was about Emry? "He hasn't been much of one lately. I know he's training..."

"He will only get busier as time goes on. If he's acting like this now, I can't even begin to imagine how he's going to be when he's king. He's going to be terrible. Terrible, like Atavia."

"She hates me," I said, trying to block out the rush of emotions he had just caused by making me think that Emry could only get worse and not better.

"Of course she does," Treyu said. "You're a human. You're after her precious baby boy."

"I'm not after him. I mean, we're together."

"Are you?"

I frowned. "Please, I think I'd rather be alone right now."

"Listen, I know I sound rude, but I just want you to really think about things. I'm not going to sugarcoat the situation for you. The way people are here, they're taught to block out their emotions.

It's a way of living and works for most people. Humans are thought to be overemotional creatures who can't control their feelings. I don't think I've ever seen anyone cry before, and it seems fitting that my first time witnessing it, it's come from a human," Treyu explained. "We've just had a head start on Emry, that's all. But now, he has his mother, who desperately wants to make up for lost time. She believes the Scaves are getting close ... too close. She needs Emry to be powerful so that if they make a move, he'll be ready for it."

"They're not getting close," I told him.

"Do you think Karn told those measly Scave kids everything? He's smarter than that, unfortunately."

Treyu grinned.

I frowned. I felt stuck here. I wanted to be on Evadere, yet I didn't. I had too many powerful people against me here, people Emry was more likely to adhere to than on Earth. After all, he had found his rightful place. He had a real family now.

"Listen," Treyu whispered, placing his hand on my knee and sliding closer. "Let me give you a bit of advice. You should find someone else to be with, someone that deserves you. Emry Logan, his ego is already going through the roof. He's not who you thought he was, and I can understand why you're upset about that, but really, people don't change. You're not going to be able to make him be someone he isn't. He's going to be king. Are you willing to be continuously pushed to the side?"

I moved my knee a little, feeling the warmth of his hand through my clothing. "The way I see it," he continued. "Emry is going to end up with someone who doesn't mind being treated like crap, because all they're going to be interested in is the power that comes along with being with him. But you, Anna James, you're the opposite. You could care less about power. You want to be treated right. I'm correct, aren't I?"

I looked up into Treyu's blue eyes. There was something devious about them. He stared back at me, his head uncomfortably close to mine, but I couldn't move. My emotions were all over the board. I wanted to run, but I knew that I should sit here and listen to Treyu no matter how much his words stung. He had a lot of logic to what he was saying. These were facts that I had needed someone to tell me, the bitter truth.

"Anna James," he whispered, his finger now under my chin and lifting my face upward. "Such an interesting human you are."

It was as if time was in slow motion as Treyu pressed his lips against mine. I felt paralyzed, unable to stop what I knew shouldn't be happening.

"He's kissing the human!" someone shrieked.

Hearing this, I pushed Treyu away and turned to see Raleigh and Emry at the doors that led back inside the castle. Emry's mouth was hanging open. He turned around and stormed back inside.

"Emry!" I called out, but he was gone.

I looked back to see Treyu skipping around the fountain, a wild look in his eyes. "Foolish humans.

Emotions *do* rule their lives. What fun to mess with them." A wicked laugh echoed off the cement as he continued to hop around.

I glared at him. How could I have let this happen? I felt the angry tears moisten my eyes. I turned away, forbidding myself to give Treyu anymore ammunition to mock my human emotions, since it was obvious he didn't have any.

Treyu's loud laughter rang out as he continued to carry on. I glanced toward the door where Emry had been, only to see the back of Raleigh's dress flutter lightly in the wind as she went back into the castle to chase after my Emry Logan.

Oh, no, I thought. *Don't even think about it, Raleigh.* My mind raced about what I was going to say to Emry when I found him, but I knew I had to say *something*. I couldn't just leave it as is, especially not with Raleigh hunting him down in a state of vulnerability. My mind kept trying to get me to return to my room to try to think things through, but jealousy overrode all other emotions at this point.

I practically ran into Jo as she rounded a corner, a tray in her hands. "Jo!" I exclaimed.

"Anna." She smiled. "I feel terrible about what happened at dinner. I'm grateful you're trying to defend me, but I really need you to know that I'm fine, *really* fine. No one is treating me badly. Look," she said, holding out her free arm. "Clean clothes. Can you believe it? Clean clothes. My hair is washed. My belly is full. I think I'm already putting on weight." She grinned.

"I know, Jo. I'm so sorry for lashing out." I didn't have time to rehash dinner's mess right now with her. "Hey, have you seen Emry? I really need to talk to him."

She pressed her lips together almost as if deciding whether or not she should tell me. She pointed down the hall. "Third room on the left, I think, but he's not alone. Raleigh ..."

"Yeah, yeah," I mumbled, rushing past her to get to the room.

The door was closed. I shut my eyes for a moment and took a deep breath. Then I thrust open the door and burst in with shame drenched all over me. Emry was sitting in a chair, his head in his hands.

Raleigh was behind him, her hands caressing his back. Anger seethed through me. Now I knew how Emry had felt only moments ago seeing me with his cousin.

Raleigh looked over her shoulder and glared at me. "I think you should leave."

I motioned toward the door. "No, it's *you* that needs to go."

"What did you just say to me?" she asked.

"It's my turn to have Emry to myself."

She put her hands on her hips. "He doesn't want to talk to you."

I exhaled loudly, unable to control the adrenaline ripping about inside me. "Emry?" I asked.

"Please, let me explain."

"Is there an explanation?" His voice was quiet.

Raleigh was still glaring at me.

"Yes. Please, let's just talk."

He didn't reply.

"I'm not discussing anything with *her* in the room." I loathed the way she was guarding him. "Raleigh, go ahead and go," Emry told her.

"You sure?" she questioned him.

"Yeah. And thanks."

We looked each other over one last time before she finally walked past me, her perfume lingering in the air momentarily as she left. I felt so much better now that she wasn't in between Emry and me.

"Can I sit beside you?" I asked, my hands shaking as I locked them together.

He still didn't look at me. He gestured toward the empty space on the couch beside him. I took a seat. I wasn't sure if I should touch his hands or not. I decided not until I could assess how much trouble I was in.

"I know what you think you saw..." I began.

"Don't play games, Anna. I saw you and Treyu lip locked. Ick," he made a disgusted noise as if he were on the verge of vomiting.

I cringed. Desperation was now taking over. "Emry, I was so upset about dinner. I went outside. He followed me. We were just talking, I promise you. *He* moved closer to me. *He* initiated the kiss. It was just someone to talk to, and I don't know what happened."

"Treyu's a jerk," he said. "I don't know how you could even stand talking to him. I can barely stomach it."

I nodded. "I know. I'm an idiot for letting him get that close. I've just had no one to talk to…"

"There's no excuse for it," he snapped. "I don't like it. I don't like you confiding in another man, especially someone like Treyu, who has absolutely no values whatsoever. I'm trying my best to balance everything, Anna. I thought, of all people, you'd understand that. I thought, of all things, our relationship wasn't something I had to worry about."

I closed my eyes. I wanted to reach out and touch him so badly, but I knew he'd only pull away if I tried. "I'm sorry." His disappointment sliced through me.

"Treyu is the son of my father's youngest brother. Mother says he's always had everything handed to him no matter what. She says he's a spoiled brat, and it shows," Emry explained.

"What about Raleigh?" I said without thinking about it.

"What about her?" He looked at me, his eyes red and puffy.

"You confide in her, and look at her."

"First of all, Anna, you have no idea if I confide in her. She's a friend of the family, and I merely entertain her when she visits."

"Which is all the time," I added.

He pressed his lips together. "You're jealous."

"Of course I'm jealous."

"Anna, you're letting your imagination get the best of you. There's nothing between us. Nothing." I narrowed my eyes. Just moments ago she was rubbing his back. "I've seen the way she looks at you. Am I imaging that, too?"

"So what, you decide to get back at me from spending time with Raleigh by making out with Treyu?"

"I didn't make out with him," I yelled. "And I already told you, *he* kissed me."

"Didn't seem like you were struggling to get away."

"Emry," I whispered, unable to hide my own tears any longer. "What's happening to us?"

He shook his head. "I think this is just too much for both of us right now."

I lowered my eyebrows. This sounded like the beginning of a breakup speech.

"I'm trying to adapt to this new world, to who I really am. I'm getting used to my powers, how to use them. This world, these people, are they really for you? You said, you had no one to talk to.

Maybe you should go give Carlin a visit, let things blow over for a while, then we'll see where we are," he suggested.

I turned away from him, biting my lip. This is exactly what Atavia wanted to happen.

"I mean, what do you want to do, Anna? Do you want to go back to Earth, or do you want to stay here? You're so unhappy here."

I couldn't believe this was happening. I had thought our hardships on Earth were going to be our last, but I had thought wrong. The ones here were even worse. I had no one to back me up. It was me against this world, this Evadere. "It's not like I see you, anyway," I admitted, knowing now he didn't want me to stay. "Do you think I'd even make it back to Earth?"

"What do you mean?" he asked, standing now and pacing around the room like he did in times of frustration.

"I just feel like she's out to get me, like she wants me dead and gone, out of the way." "Who's *she*?" he asked, narrowing his eyes as he already knew the answer.

"You're going to make me say it, aren't you?" I sighed. "Fine. Your mother."

"Come on, Anna ..."

"No, you come on. You trust her way too much and know her way too little." "She's my mother. She's protected me all these years," he said, defensively.

"And you don't think she was lying when she said I was safely back on Earth when she sent for you on the beach?"

"Well, I guess you do think she's lying."

I nodded. "I think it was absolutely her plan to leave me there. She wanted me to try to survive on Evadere alone. She knew I'd be killed."

"This is crazy talk, Anna. Seriously. You are way over-thinking what happened."

"Am I?" My anger now stirred viciously within me. Now he didn't want to be with me, and he didn't believe me. Atavia had really gotten her claws into him. Maybe Emry was too far gone to get back. "I think she's a malicious schemer. Anything to get her own way, and she wants me out of the way."

"Listen, Anna, I'm only going to tell you this one more time. I'm in training to be a king. I have big shoes to fill, my father's. There's a lot going on here between contributors and Scaves. I have to figure everything out along with my powers. I don't have time for relationship drama. I thought you'd be able to support me one hundred percent."

"I do…"

"No, not at all. You just want to stir things up and create unnecessary problems. I don't need that kind of stress right now. I need people around me who are going to lift me up, so figure out which side you stand on, Anna."

With those words, Emry Logan turned and left me all alone.

"There you are," Jillianne squealed, entering the room as she saw me standing there, still open mouthed that Emry had just left. "I've been looking everywhere for you. Come with me."

"What do you want?" I asked as she grabbed my arm like she had when she had found me in the dungeon. She pulled me toward the hallway.

"Tonight has been a mess, an absolute mess. It's time we get you back up to your room so things can settle down a bit." Jillianne led me over to the stairs. I walked with her, my body completely numb to the pressure her short, fat fingers were putting on the skin of my arm.

We got into the room where she didn't let go until I was sitting on my bed, staring up at her, unable to even care that she was being a nuisance.

"You need to calm yourself and get some sleep. Everyone's a little bit irritated, a little bit tired."

She placed a cup of warm liquid into my hands. "Now, you just drink that up and go to sleep.

Tomorrow will be a bright day for all, I just know it."

"What is it?" I asked, sniffing it, the aroma sweet and comforting.

"Something similar to what you humans would refer to as tea. Everything's all natural in it. Drink it down. Go ahead now." She put her hand under the cup and lifted it to my lips.

I eyed her, wondering if I was going to wake up in the morning if I did decide to drink this. Then again, right now I wanted to sleep. I needed to forget this evening had even happened. Maybe it'd erase my memory. Maybe I would wake up happy. I tilted the cup up so that the drink would pour into my mouth. The taste was equally sweet as the smell, like honey. It was soothing. I downed the entire thing and handed the cup back to Jillianne.

"Very good," she patted me on the head. "Get some rest," she instructed.

I watched her go, and then leaned up against one of the large pillows sitting on top of the blankets. I tried to block out all the unpleasant thoughts, of Treyu and Raleigh, of Emry's suggestion I return to Earth without him, and within minutes, I felt my lids grow heavy.

Chapter 11

A loud thumping vibrated from behind my eyes and radiated into my temples as I struggled to get my eyes to open. The light shining in from the window made the pain even more unbearable. I stretched out my arms and changed position from my side to my back. I was wet. The bed was wet. Was I sick? Had I spent the night sweating out a fever?

I sat straight up. My head lurched forward with the rest of my body. The thumping increased. I groaned. What was happening? My eyes wouldn't focus. They felt so heavy. My hands went to my dress, the same one I had worn last night. It, too, was drenched. My hand ran down my bare legs. A thick slime covered them. I brought my hands back up in front of my face and made my eyes open wider so I could get a sense of exactly what was going on.

Oh ... my ...

The dark red liquid dripped down my palms and ran down my wrists and arms. Blood. I was covered in blood. It was everywhere, all over me, all over the bed and blankets. I felt like I couldn't breathe, the pain of my lungs expanding, mixing with the extreme throbbing in my head. Was all this blood mine?

I ripped all of the blankets away from my body and turned to get out of the bed. As I tore the covers off, a bloody mess of knotted blonde hair and crimson stained porcelain skin appeared beside me. I pushed away the hair from the face. Two dead eyes stared up at me. Two eyes that belonged to Raleigh. The blood was hers. Deep gashes severed through her beautiful gown piercing into her torso.

I couldn't get out of the bed fast enough as I fell backward off the opposite edge of the mattress and collapsed onto the cool floor, my hands making blood prints in the cement. My stomach tensed up and then contracted as I vomited again and again, the force of the motion making my head feel as though it was going to split in half.

I got to my feet somehow and hobbled toward the bathroom. I turned on the shower and stripped all of the blood covered clothes to the floor. I let the hot water gush over my head and down my skin, the bottom of the tub filling with Raleigh's blood as it vanished down the drain. This couldn't be happening to me right now. Raleigh was *dead*. I was soaked in her blood as if I had tossed and turned all night with her corpse right beside me as I slept. The thought gagged me as I went to all fours again and threw up beside the drain.

I got to my feet and reached for the soap. I poured it all over my body, viciously scrubbing my skin until it burned. I had to get this off me. I couldn't stand to be covered in it. I looked down at my hands, the blood even dried under my nails. I dug them into a bar of soap and scrubbed again, my jaw clenching together from both a churning stomach and the anxiety of it all.

What was I going to do? I couldn't go back out there and see her there.

What had happened last night? I couldn't remember a thing. I remembered Jillianne giving me a drink of 'tea,' and then passing out into a deep sleep.

Think! Think! I yelled at myself. How could this have happened without my remembering a single thing? It seemed impossible, yet here it was.

I stepped out of the shower and wrapped a thick towel around me. I prayed I had gotten it all off.

Now, what to do...?

I pressed my back up against the wall and closed my eyes, attempting to think. This headache was unbelievable. I ran to the mirror and checked for injury on my head as the cause, but found nothing was there. Maybe it had been that drink. What had been in that concoction Jillianne gave me?

"Help!" I cried out. "Help me, please!" I said a little louder this time. I screamed at the top of my lungs, my skull throbbing with each shrill noise, but I knew someone had to come to me. I wasn't going out there alone to face what was left of Raleigh.

"What is it? What's wrong?" Someone I had seen at dinner a few times hurried into my room. They looked at me standing in the bathroom doorway, then looked to the pool of blood on my bed, Raleigh's arm and hand protruding from the covers. His face went white. He was an older man, short and stout. His hand moved up to his gaping mouth as he couldn't take his eyes away from the horror scene.

"Please, help me," I begged. "I don't know what happened. I just woke up and found her beside me like that. I was covered in blood. I just showered it all off, but I can't stand to go past her."

"Who is it?" he asked.

"Raleigh," I cried.

"Raleigh?"

"Yes." I sucked in a large gulp of air.

"You wait," he stuttered. "Wait right here." He put his finger up. "You wait right here, and I'll go get someone."

Tears streamed down my face. "Hurry."

The little man practically sprinted from the room.

Emry appeared at the entrance of the door. I rushed over and wrapped my arms around him. He hugged me back, my wet hair dripping all over him.

"I don't know what happened," I cried. "I didn't do this. I didn't kill Raleigh."

"Shh," he said, his hand on the back of my head so I didn't have to turn around and see her lifeless body again. "I know. I know you didn't do this. We'll get to the bottom of it. Just try to calm down."

"You believe me?" I looked up into his eyes just then.

He frowned. "Of course. I would never think you capable of murder. What's the matter with you? I'd never think such a thing."

I leaned my sobbing face against him again, unable to stop trembling.

"What's this I hear about Raleigh being dead..." I heard Atavia's voice echo down the hall and then fall short as she entered the room. I didn't want to see her. I just wanted to continue to be comforted by Emry. Ben Hanley stepped up behind Emry. I recognized his shiny shoes right away as I had been looking down. Emry turned to Ben as I stood beside him, our hands still tightly intertwined.

"Ben, get some men in here to get rid of the... body. Jillianne, go get some girls to clean this all up.

Don't even try to clean those sheets and mattress, though. Have them burned," Emry instructed everyone.

"What's *she* still doing here?" Atavia bellowed out. "Get away from my son."

I ducked behind Emry, never letting go of his hand.

"Mother, take a deep breath," Emry suggested. "This isn't what it seems."

"It's exactly what it seems," she shouted. "This girl is nothing but trouble."

"It doesn't look good," Jillianne admitted.

"Who else do you suggest we point the finger to?" Atavia asked, her voice stern and on the verge of irate.

"Not Anna. Don't even start your accusations against her. She's no killer."

"Jealousy is an emotion that can overtake any completely sensible person and turn them into a murderer," Atavia yelled. "It's one of the most, if not *the* most controlling emotion there is."

"No!" I cried out. "I did not do this!"

"Poor, poor Raleigh," Jillianne kept repeating.

"You!" I shouted. "What did you give me before bed to drink?"

"Aha!" Atavia exclaimed. "Anna was drunk, weren't you? Just look at her. She looks horrid."

"It was just a little tea-like substance to help her sleep," Jillianne explained.

I wiped the tears off my chin before they fell. "It made me black out."

"No," Jillianne said defensively. "It was nothing like you're thinking. You just slept soundly. You were exhausted."

"So soundly I don't remember Raleigh coming into my room, or dying beside me?" I questioned her. "No," I turned toward Atavia. "Someone set me up. Someone killed Raleigh and dumped her in my room to make it look like I had something to do with it."

"Unbelievable," Atavia said as men entered the room and headed to the bed to remove the corpse.

"You are the only one who would have wanted Raleigh dead. Everyone else loved her."

I looked to Emry for help. He glanced back at me, his eyes full of pity as he was just as confused as the rest of us. "Mother, stop, please. I'm telling you that Anna didn't, couldn't have done this. She's a wonderful person no matter what issues she's having with me and Raleigh. This is not the way she handles things."

The men lifted the body and began carrying her out, the blood trickling all over the floor.

"Stop," Atavia called out. "Look at what a mess you're making. You can't have a stream of blood running the whole way through the castle. I have guests."

"Your majesty?" one of the men asked.

"Put her back down. Go get something to put her in so others don't see her." She shook her head.

"Idiots." She turned to face everyone else. "Out, everyone out. You," she pointed to me. "Get dressed. I want everyone in the study. Ben, don't take your eyes off her."

"Mother, I'll stay with her," Emry offered.

"You don't know what you're saying." Atavia huffed and everyone filed out of the room.

After throwing on some clothes, I pulled my wet hair back and met Emry in the hall. He gave me a troubled look. I knew I was in for it for whatever it was that awaited me in the study with Atavia and her crew.

Jo ran up to me and grabbed my shoulders. "Anna," she hissed. She had taken me off guard. I pulled away from her grasp. "What's this I hear? You killed Raleigh?" she asked.

Emry reached out for my hand and pulled me along. "How fast rumors travel in this castle," he mumbled.

I looked back at Jo. "I didn't kill anyone."

"Don't worry about it," he whispered as we walked down the hall.

"Really?" I said. "Don't worry that others think I'm a murderer?"

He sighed, but didn't say anything else as we made a sharp turn and went into another room I'd never seen before. Everyone was eerily silent as we walked toward the front where Atavia stood.

"Tell everyone what happened," Ben said.

Everyone's face was filled with accusation and outrage as their beauty queen was dead. Of course they'd instantly think that the attention seeking, jealous girlfriend would have been the one to commit the crime.

"I don't know," I began. "I talked with Emry last night..."

"You had a fight," Jillianne corrected me.

I glared at her. "Yes, we sort of had a fight. He left, and then Jillianne came in and escorted me to my room."

"Is that true, Jillianne?" Atavia asked.

She nodded, her brown curls bobbing up and down as she did so.

"She gave me a drink to help me sleep. I fell asleep and woke up with a terrible headache. I was covered in blood with Raleigh beside me. I threw up on the floor when I realized she was dead and hurried to wash the blood away before screaming for help as I couldn't face going into that room alone again. That's it."

"Was she drunk last night, Jillianne?" Atavia asked.

"No," Jillianne said.

"Emry?"

"She was sober," he answered.

"When was the last time you saw Raleigh?" Ben asked.

This interrogation reminded me that Ben had been a lawyer on Earth. "She was with Emry when I went to talk to him. She left so we could be alone. That's the last time." I ran a hand over my smooth, wet ponytail.

"This doesn't make sense," Ben told Atavia.

"Sure it does," she snapped. "She killed her."

"How was she killed?" Emry asked. "Does anyone even know that yet?"

"Guards said Raleigh was stabbed," Ben said. "Ten times." Everyone in the room gasped.

"Poor, dear, Raleigh," Atavia whispered. "She had a fruitful life awaiting her."

I glared, knowing exactly what she meant. She had always planned on getting Emry to fall for Raleigh, to marry Raleigh.

"None of you know Anna like I do," Emry said so everyone could hear. "This nonsense of accusing her is going to stop right now." He looked around, making sure he made eye contact with everyone.

"Someone else did this. Maybe one of *you* did this."

"Emry," Atavia chastised. "You're out of line."

"Aren't I to be king?" he questioned her.

"You aren't king yet, my boy," Atavia said, a threat in her tone.

He eyed her for a moment, remaining silent. The control she had over him was so irritating. Emry was trying to defend me, to protect me for the first time since I came here. Even after all that had happened last night with Treyu, and Raleigh now dead, he was still on my side. That alone was making all this bearable, making it so I wasn't a complete wreck and not breaking down at this exact moment.

Ben stepped next to Atavia. "My queen," he said, lowering his head and giving her a little bow.

"What do you propose?"

She put a finger to her lips and tapped it there a few times. She glanced at Emry and then me. "Someone hasn't been killed in the castle since King Calan was murdered by Karn," I heard someone whisper from behind me. I knew Emry had heard it, too. The side of his jaw tightened in tension.

Atavia consulted with Ben quietly for a few moments so that no one else could hear.

Ben turned away from her and faced us. "The queen has decided an investigation has to take place to determine the facts. Once the facts are found out, they will be made public immediately."

Atavia whispered something to him again.

"Yes," he agreed. "Please, no one needs to panic. No one is in danger. The guards will be put on high alert for any unusual behavior, so just go about your usual business for the rest of the day."

"Am I off the hook?" I whispered to Emry.

"I wouldn't say that," he replied. "I guess things can't ever be simple around this place. Come on, let's go find you another room. Unless..."

I narrowed my eyes at him.

"You want to still sleep in that same room?" he asked.

"Real funny," I whispered. "What an appropriate time for humor, Emry."

He shrugged and we filed out of the room, along with everyone else.

"Anna? Anna? Are you awake?"

The doors to my new room opened and Ben hurried inside. I sat up in bed as I was still trying to recover from the headache that was just now starting to subside. "I don't know if I'll be able to sleep ever again."

He smoothed out his dark-colored coat with his hands as he stood in front of me. "I need you to get up. How do you look? Put on something decent."

"What's going on?" I got out of bed and hurried over to the closet in search of something to wear.

He shook his head. "What a mess. Raleigh's family has just arrived at the castle."

"What?" I asked, my eyes widening at the thought. "What do you want with me?"

"They're demanding to see you."

I turned around to face him, the fear already starting to make my hands quiver.

"It'll be alright," he assured me. "No one is going to harm you. I'll be there, along with Emry.

They're quarreling with the queen right now."

I walked into the main entrance of the castle where Raleigh's family, an older man, three younger men, and a woman, stood. I supposed them to be her parents and brothers. They looked livid, the three younger men holding spears in their hands but not aiming them, and the woman's head was covered in a veil, tissues clutched tightly in her hands as she dabbed her nose every now and then.

"Ben," Atavia said in relief. "There you are." She looked my way.

"Is that her?" one of the younger men asked. "Is that the human?"

I folded my hands together, my eyes not moving away from the spears. These contributors were here to avenge Raleigh's death. They wanted answers, but no one could give them.

"This is her," Atavia said, gesturing toward me.

Both Ben and Emry stepped in front of me at the same time.

"Why do you protect her?" the older man lashed out. "Why are you hoarding humans and Scaves here, anyway? Are you turning against us, my queen?"

"Watch your tongue, Omelius," Ben warned. "The queen's powers outweigh your own."

"My daughter has been slaughtered here," the man reminded him. "I have every right to know what's going on."

"We don't know what happened yet," Ben said. "There's an investigation underway as we speak."

One of the younger men spit on the floor. "Who needs an investigation? We were told the human did it."

"She did not," Emry said.

"This is an outrage. I demand you kill her right now, or we will," he told Emry.

"Again, I'd watch what you say," Ben said. "You haven't met him yet, but this is your future king." Raleigh's mother's eyes widened at the news as she examined Emry from head to toe. "This is your Son; the one you promised my Raleigh to marry?"

Emry and Atavia exchanged glances. Emry hadn't known his mother's intentions for Raleigh, just as I had suspected. Raleigh had been nothing more but a pawn in the queen's game of making choices for Emry's life here on Evadere.

Atavia chuckled. "Who knows if it would've worked out?"

The woman glared at her.

"Why is this human here, anyway? How did she get here?" one of the brothers asked.

"It's not really any of your business," Atavia snapped.

"Oh, just tell them, Mother," Emry said. "There's no use in making things worse than they already are. My deepest sympathies to you and your family, sir. Raleigh was a wonderful woman, one you raised properly. I had no idea that she was here to court me," Emry explained. "This *human,* as you refer to her, is Anna James. She's here because of me. I'm in love with her."

The family gasped. Even Atavia was shocked that he had admitted such a thing. What an embarrassment it had to have been for her. I couldn't help the smirk that crossed my lips.

"I'm afraid I don't understand," Raleigh's mother said softly.

"I was hidden away on Earth for my entire life up until now," he explained. "I interacted with the humans. I lived as a human. I had human relationships; this one being the most vital. That's all you need to know about the situation. She didn't kill Raleigh. This whole thing was meant to look as if she did."

The family exchanged glances with one another.

"Then who did?" the man asked.

"As I said," Ben answered, "there's an investigation ..."

"The human did it," Atavia said, interrupting Ben. "Emry doesn't think so, because he's not looking at the situation logically but emotionally. No one is going to convince me otherwise."

One of the brothers pointed his spear at me.

"Why do these men still have weapons in our castle?" Emry questioned the guards and his mother.

"Take their weapons away."

Raleigh's brothers stood in a defensive manner. They put their backs together so their weapons were all facing outward as the guards surrounded them.

"Enough!" Atavia yelled. "Hasn't enough blood been shed for one day?" She put her hands on her hips.

"Humans and Scaves ... seems like more should be shed to me," one of the brothers stated.

"They're not welcome here."

"Who are you to judge the queen?" Ben asked.

"Our daughter is dead," the woman said, sobbing. "We are grieving. Why can you not understand that?"

"This is not the proper way to grieve," Ben informed her. "She could have you all locked away for this."

"If she did, more contributors would come to avenge us, that is certain," Raleigh's father assured everyone.

Atavia's face had twisted up as she kept her distance from Raleigh's family. "Guards, go get Raleigh's body. Hurry."

We all waited in silence, everyone staring at one another, everyone posed for battle. The guards returned in minutes, carrying a large white bundle that held the once stunning Raleigh. They dumped her body carelessly on the floor in front of her family.

The mother gasped at the harshness of the guards. She rushed to the covered body and threw herself over it.

"Pigs!" one of the brothers shouted.

"Enough," Atavia commanded. "Gather your child and be gone. You are not welcome here again." Everyone eyed each other one last time before the father picked up his dead child in his arms and the group of contributors left, Raleigh's elegant presence tainted by a gory one of a pool of cooled blood on my bed.

"I want extra security around the clock," Atavia told the guards. "I want every entrance guarded.

Am I understood?"

"Yes, your majesty," they replied, almost in unison.

Atavia's cheeks were flushed, her always perfect hair now disheveled as pieces fell down on the sides. She rubbed the front of her neck with one hand, the other on her waist. "I want that human locked up. I want her thrown in the dungeon where she belongs."

One of the guards stepped toward me.

Emry tensed for battle. "No. You're upset by the contributors."

"In all this time, in all these years, never have I had a group of contributors waltz in here and try to call the shots," she mumbled. "No one has ever been murdered in my castle. Not since..." she hesitated.

"Father?" Emry asked.

Atavia swallowed. Thinking about her dead husband actually made emotion surface on the queen's face. Perhaps she had really loved Calan, and still did to this day. "Yes, since that incident." Then her face tightened as she pointed her finger at me. "None of these things would've happened if *she* hadn't come along. She's a problem, Emry, I'm telling you."

"You just want someone to blame. She hasn't done anything," Emry said, defending me once again. I stepped closer to him and wrapped my fingers into his, but he jerked his hand away, his back still turned as he stood in front of me. Why had he pulled away from me like that? I took two steps away from him.

"This is the first act of rebellion, I can feel it," Atavia rambled on. "No one's going to want to be a guest here anymore. They'll all be afraid for their lives. They'll be afraid of the Scave maidservants, of the human."

"Mother..."

"Emry, she has to be out of our lives. Don't you see what she's doing? She's tearing our kingdom apart, little by little. She's a demon who's weaseled her way in. I can't just stand here and let her ruin you, ruin us. She has to be put in the dungeon so I know everyone's safe."

"No," he said sternly.

"Then let's exile her to Earth. Put her back with her kind. You'll forget her soon enough. There are women lining up just to speak with you," Atavia continued, trying to be persuasive. "We'll look back on this and laugh at the time you thought you loved a human." She laughed then.

"She can hear you, you know." Emry turned to me. "No one will do any harm to Anna, or they'll have to answer to me. Ben, protect her." With that, he began walking at a fast pace down the hall.

I stood there for a few moments, watching after him before I hurried to catch up. "Emry," I called out. "Please wait."

His steps seemed to speed up, so I sprinted after him. "Please!" I yelled.

Emry stopped dead in his tracks. I practically ran into him as he turned around to look at me. "What is it?" he asked.

I lowered my eyebrows, trying to read his red and tired eyes. "What's wrong? Don't you want to be around me now? I thought …"

"Anna, listen," he said. "A lot is going on. Everything's a mess. It feels like I have all these pieces I have to put back together again. I'm stressed out. I can't sleep. Raleigh was just murdered in a place I'm supposed to call home. Everyone's against the idea of you and me. It's just a lot right now. Can't you understand that?"

The tone of his voice frightened me. "Of course, Emry, I understand, but…"

"Now I have to try and make amends with Raleigh's family so my mother won't be so paranoid that more people are out to get her. She's already paranoid enough as it is about the Scaves since I've been back."

"I'm sorry things haven't exactly gone as planned for you," I whispered. "I'm sorry you feel I'm not there for you."

"It's fine. I'm fine," he said in a harsh tone. "I'm used to being on my own, remember? It's just before, when things got tough, I transported here. Now where do I go?"

I shook my head, realizing what he must be going through. A lot had changed for him, and now, all of a sudden, he was in charge of all these contributors with all these problems. He had a mother that thrived on her powers and ability to get others to do as she said. Our relationship was on the back burner, compared to all of these things right now. I had to give him space again. At least he had stood up for me against his mother in front of everyone. That had to mean *something*.

"I just need to be alone right now, okay?" he asked.

I nodded, but not fully understanding.

"It's like I'm being pulled in all these different directions. I've just never had this kind of responsibility before. It's crazy. I'm not used to any of this, and suddenly people are looking to me for answers. I'll figure it out." He stared at me for a moment longer before turning to go. I watched as he made it a few steps and then turned back around. "Who do *you* think killed Raleigh?"

I hesitated for a moment. "I honestly think Atavia did it so she could have an excuse to get rid of me, get me away from you."

"You two are unbelievable." He clenched his jaw together and glared at me before storming off. I watched him walk through the side doors that led to the outside. He lifted his arm up in the air and an entire wall near the fountain crumbled to the ground.

Chapter 12

The next few days were dull and spent in my room. I would leave and go to the library and get some books on the planet's history. I would read until I felt sleepy and then nap. I was no longer called for dinner. Meals were always brought to my room.

I stared out the window and sighed. It was nighttime now. The less I did, the more tired I became. It was a vicious cycle. I wasn't sure what I was supposed to do. Should I stay here and wait, and if so, what exactly was it that I was waiting for? Then again, if I returned to Earth, what would I do there? I knew all I'd think about was Emry, and at least here I knew we were on the same planet. Emry hadn't transported back to Earth since leaving the beach. I mean, why would he? There was nothing back there for him and everything here.

I thought about Atavia's intentions and how I was glad that Lainey Tritt was the one that supposedly raised him instead of her. I was a little shocked that she permitted her baby prince to be around someone like Lainey and her living arrangements, compared to this lavish castle.

Carlin's face entered my mind. It had been a long time since I'd thought of her. Right before returning to Evadere with Emry, she had found herself a new job and a new man. She was living on the outskirts of Seneca and traveling to a nearby city to work. She seemed happy. I had been staying with her for awhile before finding my own place, a small apartment near Emry. I had barely even spent any time in the new apartment before all this happened.

Carlin had seemed very happy. I think the burden of letting me know the big secret that she was my biological mother had been lifted. She was like a new woman. It was great to see her actually smile and enjoy life. She had been packing for a cruise she was going on with her boyfriend the last time I had seen her. She'd be back from the cruise by now. I wondered if she was thinking about me, if she was worried where I was. I sighed and walked over the bed and plopped down.

Then I thought about my brother, Matthew. He was still living with Helene and John, my step-parents who had taken care of me in Carlin's stead. I hadn't had much contact with them after Emry was been released from prison. That also meant little contact with Matthew. I thought about him sitting in front of the TV, and smiled. It seemed ages ago when I was in that house. What a boring life I had led before Emry Logan. Now look at me. I am on Evadere, surrounded by contributors and Scaves. My boyfriend was soon to be king, and his powers were getting stronger. He had proved that with his little temper tantrum knocking the wall down.

Then there was Atavia, whom I was no match against. She had the same powers as Emry as soon as she married Calan. She had wanted Raleigh to have those kinds of powers, but her plan failed.

Perhaps she had been angry with Raleigh and decided to kill her, with the strategy to pin the whole thing on me. I shuddered at the thought of seeing Raleigh's bloody corpse beside me in bed and wrapped my arms around my knees.

I felt homesick and a little lonely. I wasn't sure what exactly I was homesick for, though. Certainly not Seneca, Ohio. I was sad as I wanted things between Emry and me to be how they were before. Evadere was supposed to be this special place, a paradise. Emry and I had planned to explore the land together. It was going to be wonderful. Instead this place had become a nightmare full of both contributors and Scaves alike trying to kill me. Now I was dealing with a queen that was out to get me as well. Atavia was more powerful than Mrs. Anderson. I feared for my life even more. Here, she could keep her eye on me. She kept everyone in the palm of her hand, even the contributors, as she invited different ones daily to dine with her at the castle and show them a good time. She pretended to be friends with them, in case she needed them for a war against the Scaves. Now she needed Emry to take her lead and do exactly as she was doing. This meant he needed to believe exactly what she believed. I supposed she figured that keeping him on Earth would mean he'd gain no real human values of his own since Earth was despised and looked down upon. But I knew better. Emry was his own person. He hadn't detached himself emotionally as most people on Evadere had. That's what he had gained as being raised as a human. I couldn't let him forget that no matter how hard Atavia would try to convince him otherwise. She had obviously loved her husband. You could see the pain on her face whenever Calan was mentioned. I believed she loved Emry, too, but had bigger plans for him that overrode her motherly duty.

She wanted to conform him to be the kind of king his father had been. I wondered if she had had control of Calan, or what kind of person she had been around him. Now she seemed so hardened, so determined to get what she wanted out of Emry's presence here. It made me fear for what was going to happen between the contributors and Scaves.

I thought of the Scave people and how their rugged lives had transformed them into scavenging beasts of the land. They had every right to be angry, but Karn was very much like Atavia as far as leadership goes. He was building up his own army as well. Though significantly smaller, his people were true survivors, their pain threshold high and their determination one that had been passed on throughout the years as they knew nothing except persecution.

Surely my life was in more danger than even I could imagine. They were merely tolerating my presence for the sake of Emry. I truly believed Atavia didn't think I had even the slightest chance of making it back to him from the beach alive, but I did. Now I was in the middle of this big mess. My own helplessness began to drive me crazy the more I was left alone in this room to think freely with nothing else to occupy myself with.

The next day, I got up early, got dressed, and decided I needed to get out of here and escape my own thoughts. I walked toward the outside garden where I had seen Emry knock over the wall.

There was a chill to the air as I walked around barefoot. The wall was still missing, but the mess Emry had made had been cleaned up.

I heard men hollering and clangs of metal striking metal. Feeling cold, I wrapped my arms around myself and made my way over to the edge of where the wall had been, and peered down.

Several of Atavia's guards were standing in a circle. In the middle of that circle stood Emry. He was holding a long, metal weapon of some sort and was fighting several of the guards at one time.

The guards wore heavy armor and helmets to protect themselves. They were about the same height as Emry, but broader and overall larger men. Emry, on the other hand, was wearing loose white pants and was shirtless with nothing to protect him.

It took me a moment to process what was going on. This had to be part of Emry's training. A tree stood a little distance from the area where the men were. Atavia, with a long black dress fluttering about in the chilled wind, stood by it.

I ducked down behind the edges of the bricks still intact near the bottom of the wall as I didn't want Atavia to see me. My attention returned to Emry, who was still sparring with the guards taking them on two by two. His weapon would collide with the guards', and the whole process would begin again.

"Again," Atavia commanded.

With that, Emry lifted his metal staff high in the air and attacked another man on his side. Another guard snuck up from behind him and knocked Emry to the ground. Emry grunted in frustration, lying there for a few moments.

"Again," Atavia said in the same strict tone. "Get up, Emry."

He scrambled to his feet and stretched out his arms and shoulders before the guards surrounded him again. I found myself biting on my fingernails, nervous just watching all of this, even if it wasn't a real battle. Atavia was making him into a soldier, one man against many. I wondered how many days Emry had been practicing this.

He swung his staff back and let out another yell as he charged the man in front of him. The weapons made a loud noise as they connected fiercely, Emry obviously releasing his frustrations. I saw Atavia raise her arm in the air, gesturing something to someone.

Just then, two guards came up to Emry from behind and grabbed his arms, his weapon falling to the ground. Now he was defenseless. His anger exploded as he viciously thrashed his body about, trying to get the men off him, but it was no use. They were stronger than him.

Then Emry cried out and all of the guards, including those who had been standing back just observing the battle, flew up into the air a good height and came crashing back down on the ground, their armor making a loud thud as they landed. Emry still stood in the middle of them, his chest heaving up and down as he made attempts to calm his labored breathing. He had used his powers to defeat them all. I stood there bewildered at what had just happened, at what Emry had just made happen. I know it was considered normal here, but it was still freakish to my measly human mind.

Atavia clapped as she proceeded to leave the side of the tree and go stand near her son. She put her hand on his shaky shoulder and whispered something to him. He was now slouched over, drained from what had just occurred.

A high-pitched scream came from within the castle. I turned and sprinted toward the noise. My footsteps slowed as I reached the hallway where a small crowd had already gathered outside a room. I tried to see who was inside, but there were too many blocking my field of vision.

Emry, Atavia, and the guards made it there seconds after me. "Move aside," Atavia yelled out. "Go on, get ... get, I said."

They moved out of the way so that the queen and her crew could get through and into the room.

Emry peered at me out of the corner of his eye. I snuck in behind him so I could get into the room, too.

In the corner of the room kneeled a girl, still squealing as loud as she could, her face buried in her hands. Across the room behind a large desk the feet of someone lying behind the massive piece of furniture stuck out.

"That's enough of that," Atavia scolded the maidservant, who instantly silenced herself at the voice of the queen. "What is going on...?"

We moved together in a small group over to the pair of feet that belonged to the stout body of Jillianne. She was dead, her glazed over eyes staring toward the ceiling as a small pool of blood pillowed behind her head, the handle of a knife protruding from her gashed neck.

"Jillianne!" Atavia cried out, bending down and touching her head that lifelessly fell to the side, a trickle of blood exiting from her tipped mouth. Atavia now cried out in disgust as she jumped back in alarm. Her eyes were alit with fury as she stood up straight. She clenched her jaw together very much in the same way that Emry did when he was upset. She looked back to the maidservant still huddled in the corner. "You," she shouted, pointing to the girl. "What happened? Tell me what you saw."

The girl began to tremble as she bit her lip, trying too hard not to start screaming again in fear of what the queen might do if she was unable to get hold of herself.

"I ... I ..." the maidservant stuttered.

Atavia raised her eyebrows, her emotions becoming more and more composed by the second. "Get up and speak!"

The poor girl kept shaking all over as she made an attempt to get to her feet, but failed miserably as she fell against the wall. No one was helping her, so I walked over and gave her a hug.

"It's ok," I whispered to her. "No one's going to hurt you. Did you find Jillianne like this?"

She nodded.

"Okay," I whispered. "Just get up and tell the queen what happened. That's all she wants from you."

I offered the maidservant my hand, which she accepted, and pulled her to her feet. Then I stood by her side as she faced Atavia, who was now glaring at me.

"I'm waiting," she told the maidservant. "And I'm not a very patient person."

"I ... just came in here to clean, your majesty. And Ms. Jillianne ..." The maidservant's eyes floated back over toward the corpse, causing her to crumble emotionally again.

Atavia's shoe clicked on the hard floor.

"Ms. Jillianne was just like that already. She was dead," the girl managed to say.

Atavia's hands went to her face momentarily. Then she looked up, her face seemingly aged in her distress. "Get out," she snapped. "Everyone out. Get out of my castle."

The crowd scrambled to get away from Atavia's anger and Jillianne's spilled blood. I could only imagine what the contributors were saying about the death of Raleigh at the castle and now another one.

"Guards, get this mess cleaned up," Atavia commanded.

I glanced up at Emry, who was standing near Ben, both of them in disbelief and unsure of what to say to the queen, probably afraid she was about to go off. I turned to leave. I wanted no part of her temper.

"Where do you think *you're* going?" she yelled.

I was thrown against the wall, my arms pinned behind my back by some unknown force. I couldn't move. My spine hurt from the force of hitting the wall. I glared at Atavia. She had used her powers on me. It was both extraordinary and infuriating at the same time.

Emry took two steps toward me, and then stopped. "Mother ..."

"I don't even want to hear your opinion, Emry, which by the way, is so completely tainted. Humans are known for their bloodshed," Atavia scolded him. "Your judgment is impaired when it comes to anything dealing with this girl."

He ran his fingers through his hair and took a deep breath. "Let her down."

"She murdered Jillianne!" she cried out.

"What?" I shouted. "You think I did this? I wasn't anywhere near here. I was outside watching Emry train with your guards."

"Do you have witnesses?" she asked, her tone on the verge of mockery.

I glared at her again and tried to move. It was a worthless attempt. My arms were beginning to ache from being squished between the wall and my body.

"Why would she want to kill Jillianne?" Emry questioned.

The guards glanced up momentarily at us before lifting the body onto a large canvas and carrying it out of the room. This seemed to disturb Atavia further.

"She's human. I want her locked in the dungeon immediately."

"Out of the question," Emry said, his tone calm and controlled.

I wanted to scream at her that I thought she was capable of doing it, that maybe Jillianne had crossed her somehow and she was pinning this whole thing on me to get me away from Emry, but I couldn't make the words come out of my mouth. She had strong powers, and I didn't know the extent of them, but I didn't doubt that she could kill me if she wanted to, or if she lost all control, which by the look on her face, wasn't far from happening.

"She killed that woman in the courthouse back on Earth," Atavia quickly pointed out. "That woman was coming after me," Emry snapped.

"Without hesitation, *she* killed her."

Emry's eyes narrowed. "Or I'd be dead."

Atavia let out a huffing noise.

"You just don't like her," Emry said. "Your judgment is impaired because of your dislike. Someone else did this."

"Who?" she screamed. She turned around and looked at Ben, who shrugged his shoulders. He didn't seem to have anything to say.

"Ow," I mumbled, trying to wriggle my wrists.

Emry shot me a glance. "You're hurting her. Let her down."

Atavia's fingers massaged her temples.

I felt whatever force was holding me, slowly release. I fell to the floor. Emry came over and helped me up.

"You okay?" he whispered.

I nodded.

"I can't think with her here," Atavia confessed.

"Mother, she's innocent," Emry continued.

Atavia didn't seem capable of listening to reason anymore. "Something is wrong here. Something is wrong ..."

Emry put his hand on my back and slowly led me out of the room. Then I smacked into what seemed like a wall that wasn't really there. Emry looked back at me. Atavia had done it again. His mother was holding her hand pointed at me.

"Dungeon, murderer," she growled.

Emry clenched his jaw together. "Okay, Mother, listen—you need space. You need to grieve your friend."

"Jillianne worked for me," she said.

"Whatever," Emry continued. "Anna will stay in her room for a while."

"Emry, no ..." I started to say, but he stopped me.

"She won't leave. She'll be watched. Just compromise with me on this. What do you say?" he asked.

She stared at me for a few seconds. "Ben ..."

"I'm on it," Ben replied. "I'll make sure she goes nowhere."

"Ben's going to escort you upstairs," Emry told me. "I need to speak with the queen."

Atavia released her hold on me yet again, and I walked out of the room, Ben right behind me.

When we reached the base of the steps, I felt my stomach clench up, as if I were going to the dungeon. "Ben, I can't be locked in that room."

"I don't know what to tell you at this point. Room or dungeon, take your pick. Queen Atavia has been through a lot lately. I don't need her pushed over the edge," Ben told me.

I sighed. "But you don't understand ..."

He turned around and bent down to look me straight in the eye. "Anna, this castle is pure chaos right now. I don't think you're a murderer. Is that what you need to hear?"

"I appreciate your being on my side and all..."

"That doesn't mean I'm on your side." Ben pressed his lips together and straightened out his back again. "I work for the Queen. Just because I believe you're innocent doesn't make me your friend."

I swallowed. "You're going to make me go back to that room, aren't you?"

He nodded.

I gave in and followed him up the stairs. I went back into the room and turned around to look at Ben, who lingered for a few seconds.

"If there's nothing else you need..." he said.

I felt the tears threaten to come. I thought I might explode if he left; the emptiness already too much to bear. "Ben, wait."

He turned his head, his annoyance of watching over me clearly shown. I knew he had a lot to handle right now and my emotional state was far from a concern of his. "Could you please get Emry for me? I need to speak with him. Right now."

He stared at me for a few more moments before nodding and turning to go.

The door shut and I couldn't move. I stood there and looked at it. My mind swirled with the picture of the guards carrying out Jillianne's limp body. I wrapped my arms around my ribs and hugged myself. My eyes wandered around the walls of the room where heavy curtains hung to the floors, a great spot for someone to hide out and wait … wait for me to sit down, lay down, turn my back, anything just so they could sink a knife into me. I was sure I wasn't the only one feeling the paranoia right now. Someone had killed

Raleigh and Jillianne, and whether it was the same person or not, someone had access here in the castle. I felt vulnerable. I doubted Ben would make watching me as his top priority. Why hadn't I made him search the room before he left? Why hadn't he thought of that himself?

My nerves were getting the best of me. I looked around the dimly lit room for something to use as a weapon. I couldn't find anything suitable. I rushed over to the curtains and ripped them back. Nothing. My heart pounded as I walked to the other side of the room to the other window and did the same thing. Again, nothing. I flipped the light on in the bathroom, my hands trembling. No one was here.

I walked back out to the bedroom and over to the door. I turned the knob. Ben had locked me in. I covered my face with my hands and let the tears fall. I leaned my back against the door and let my body slump down to the floor. This stuck feeling was one of the worst ones I had ever experienced. I didn't belong on Evadere. I didn't belong on Earth. Emry was the only one I wanted to be with, and now everything was a giant mess with our relationship, with his relationship with his newly-found mother. Nothing made sense, and I felt so useless. There wasn't one thing to concentrate on. I couldn't help Emry. I couldn't help figure out who had killed Raleigh, or Jillianne, or what the motive was.

Everyone thought I was a threat, no matter what I said. Emry didn't, but now wasn't a good time to be working on *us*.

I couldn't do anything locked in this room. I was going to lose my sanity this way. Me alone with my thoughts was not a good thing. All I felt was self-pity. I was wallowing in it. I leaned my head against the door and closed my eyes.

Someone knocked on the door. The sudden noise startled me as I clambered away from it on my hands and knees.

Chapter 13

"Anna?"

The door opened. It was Emry. I hurried to get to my feet, the tears still streaming down my cheeks.

He walked over and hugged me, his warm chest against my cheek.

"This is too much for you," he whispered, his arms gripping me tighter. "Look how upset you are. I never wanted this for you."

I looked up into his blue eyes, now clouded with the wreckage of a castle that was being handed over for him to take care of. He wiped away the dampness on my face with the palms of his hands.

"I don't know what to do about this, about us," he said. It sounded so honest, it hurt. "I have to deal with my mother, who is very unstable at the moment. Ben said he's only seen her like this one other time, when my father was killed and she had to send me to Earth."

I understood, I really did, but I wished I didn't. This just wasn't working with us. He was trying to become this great king, and I had to be locked up in a room. I was just another nuisance to add to his huge list of problems. I wasn't helping matters by being here.

"Emry," I whispered, choking on the lump forming in my throat. "I'm so confused right now."

"Me too, me too," he agreed.

"But I do know that I can't stay here anymore, not like this."

He nodded. His hair fell forward and he instinctively pushed it away with his fingers. He avoided making eye contact with me as he pulled away.

"There are things going on here," I continued. "Things detrimental to people's lives. Evadere is a place on the verge of war. It's not fair for me to wage war on you, too, which is what I feel like I'm doing."

"No, it's my mother..."

I took his hand and stared at his fingers. Then I looked up at him again. He was still staring at the floor. "You've found family. You've discovered who you really are. I'm so happy for you."

"I'm sorry I've been ignoring you. I didn't mean to..."

"I'm not looking for you to make me feel better. The truth is: I feel horrible. I feel like I've caused you more problems that you should've had to deal with. If only I would have known and wouldn't have tried to come here," I said, more tears slipping from my eyes.

"No one could've known all this was in my future."

"Or your past," I added.

He grinned. "Yeah, really."

"Emry, I'm going to leave you to deal with all of this. I don't want to be a distraction anymore. I don't want to keep coming between you and Atavia," I said.

His eyebrows lowered in concern as he looked at me. I wondered if he was feeling as much pain at this moment in his gut, in his chest, in each breath he inhaled and exhaled, as I did.

"What do you want to do, then?" he asked.

I bit my bottom lip. This was the hardest thing I'd ever had to say. I had thought starting out here on Evadere that it was just me and Emry against the world, against any world. "I want you to take me back to Earth."

"I think that's the best thing, too," he whispered.

Wow, I thought. He didn't even try to stop me. This had to have been in his head before I suggested it. Did he even realize that if this happened, which it would, that I doubted I'd ever see him again?

This could possibly be our very last personal conversation with each other, and he was avoiding even touching me.

"You know, maybe spend some time with Carlin. She's probably worried sick."

"You've thought about Carlin?" I asked, surprised. I had barely thought about her.

He shrugged. "Take a break from all this." He spread his arms in the air and looked around the room. "Get to know your mother."

"While you get to know yours," I said, feeling as if I were going to puke.

"Yeah."

"Get to know our mothers..." The words floated off my tongue. "And never get to know you." These words struck him as he shot me a glance.

"You're the one who said you wanted to go."

"And you agreed with me," I added.

Emry began pacing around the room the way he always did when his mind was going full throttle, his temper peaking along with his thoughts. "You want to stay here locked in this room, then fine, have at it."

"It's absolutely ridiculous that I'm locked up in this room," I yelled. "You know I don't deserve this."

"Right. You don't deserve any of this, which is why you need to go back to Earth. That's the reason I agreed."

"We don't spend any time together. Atavia is always putting me down." I watched him pace. I could feel the emotions bundling up within me. I didn't want to have a fight.

"It's not my fault, Anna. I need to be properly trained..." "Atavia has put all of this in your head to keep us apart."

"You don't like her," he accused me.

"She doesn't like me," I replied, my voice rising.

There was a knock on the door. Emry glared at me before opening it. "Everything okay in here?" It was Ben.

"Fine, Ben," Emry answered, shutting the door again and turning back to me. "I'll take you back then."

I closed my eyes for a few moments, trying to block out the pain of his words, the harshness that his voice had turned into. "When?"

Emry walked over to the window and peered out. "After the execution."

"What?" What was he talking about? "Who's being executed?"

A smirk crossed his lips as I could see he found delight in whoever it was. He turned around and stared into my eyes. "Mrs. Anderson."

"What?" I said. This new information shocked me.

"She's been after me for a long time, as you're well aware of," he explained.

I struggled to process it. Had this been his decision? Atavia's? "She's in the dungeon, though," I said. "She can't hurt you down there."

"Yeah, but she can't stay there forever."

"So you're going to kill her?"

"It's an execution, Anna," he corrected me, his blue eyes dark in the delightfulness of destroying an enemy.

"Oh, I'm sorry," I told him. "I thought execution *was* killing."

He sighed. "I actually thought that's the one thing you'd understand."

"No, I don't. You're not the person I thought you were. Emry Logan on Earth, is not Emry Logan on Evadere."

His face showed a hint of pain from my comment.

"This world was supposed to be beautiful, magical. It just seems like everyone's hands have blood on them here. Everyone kills so freely. It's justified somehow in their minds, but to me, it's murder nonetheless."

"Mrs. Anderson is a threat to *me*. She has tried to kill *me*. She's a danger in the dungeon, out of the dungeon, on Earth, on Evadere," he said.

I nodded. "Right. So just get rid of her."

"Yes," he said, smugness showing through. "So she'll no longer be a burden. Ben is in agreement with this, too, and she's his sister."

"Oh." I rolled my eyes. "I guess since Ben thinks it's okay, then it is okay."

"Look what she did to you, in her basement," he reminded me.

I thought about the time I had been viciously tossed down Mrs. Anderson's basement stairs by her son and then kept there as a prisoner while they tried to keep me from interfering with Emry's trial. I was severely injured and kept in dirty conditions until Carlin came for me and released me from Mrs. Anderson's grip.

"You'll have more enemies than just Mrs. Anderson. Do you plan on killing them also?"

He narrowed his eyes as if the thought had never crossed his mind before. "If it comes down to it; and if you're referring to the Scaves, don't think I'm not going straight for Karn's throat. He murdered my father in front of my mother."

I really didn't want to stay here and watch the blood bath any longer. I would be sad to leave

Emry, devastated even, but at the same time, this kind of revenge was not something I could condone. "I don't want to be here for Mrs. Anderson's execution," I told him.

He ran his fingers through his hair and then his hand rested at his hips. "It's happening in a few days. It's something I need to train for. I need to save my energy and not use it on transporting, so just enjoy a few more days in Evadere."

"Locked in this room?" I raised my eyebrows.

He shook his head as if I were being impossible. "Mrs. Anderson is a traitor to the royal family.

She has always been after destroying the royal blood. She will be destroyed first, and this will be a lesson to others who may have similar ideas, to the Scaves even. That's why it will be a public execution."

Yes, it was all justified in his mind. Atavia had twisted his way of thinking. He was turning into the son she had always wanted all these years. He was conforming into her puppet.

"I have nothing left to say," I admitted, my determination crushed by Atavia's reign on her son. She wasn't even present, and yet her hold was still so strong.

"Okay then," he said. "Right after the execution, I'll take you back."

I nodded and watched as he opened the door and slammed it behind him.

I heard the door creak as my eyes fluttered open in the dark. Someone turned on a lamp and came over to the bed where I had been in and out of sleep for hours.

"Hey."

I looked up into the face of Jo. She sat down beside me. "What time is it?" I asked.

"Early morning," Jo said in a whisper. "I was just getting ready for the day. I heard you had to stay up here, so I thought I'd stop in."

"Oh, Jo," I said, feeling so pathetic but having had no one to talk to at all here. "This place is pure hell for me. Everyone's against me. Everyone's against the idea of Emry and me. Now they think I'm a murderer."

"It's easy to blame an outsider," Jo whispered. "I'm sorry everything didn't turn out the way you had pictured it in your mind."

I chuckled. "Yeah, I never pictured Emry Logan being the king of another planet. I mean, I knew he had powers, but all of this, and this castle and his mother ..."

"Yeah," she said. I could tell she really did sympathize with me.

"I'm the one who's sorry. I got you in the middle of this mess by having you bring me here. Now Rooney is gone ..."

"I miss Rooney," Jo admitted. "But not Karn. I hope I never see him again."

I sighed and sat up in the bed. "Jo, I have to tell you something." I paused to look at her. She looked different. Her face was filling out from all the nutrients she was now receiving from eating properly.

She looked healthy and had clean clothes on. Her hair was pulled neatly back. "I'm leaving."

She looked down at her hands. "Going back to Earth?"

"Yeah. I can't stay here any longer than I have to."

She remained quiet.

"Do you want to come with me?" I asked.

She looked up at me then, her eyes big and round in alarm. The thought terrified her. "To Earth?"

"Yes, to Earth."

"Anna, I can't. I'm a Scave."

"Actually, Jo, I bet you'd fit in there better than here. We could be roommates. I'd teach you all about humans. No one has powers there."

She kept staring at me, as if trying to decipher whether I was a lunatic or not. "I really like it here." "Serving Atavia?" I wrinkled my nose.

"I know she can be mean sometimes, but so was Karn. I get fed here. I have a nice bed. The other maidservants are really nice to me, despite who I am. I'm just not as brave as you, Anna."

"You're much braver than me. I can't believe you'd even say such a thing. You left all that you knew to come here," I reminded her.

She twisted up her lips. "Only because I had to. I have no other choice but to leave, or die at the hand of Karn. I can't go to another planet. I just want to stay here," she said. And there was that shy girl I had first met on the beach. A shy girl with an enormous solider within her.

I patted her hand. "Alright then, Jo. You stay here. Are you going to be okay?"

"You're not coming back?" she asked, her eyes growing large again.

I looked away from her. "I don't know. I really doubt it. Emry's life is here, and with Atavia in the picture, his life can't have me in it."

"You need to fight, Anna."

"I've tried. I talked to Emry about all this. It's decided. It's what's best, really."

Jo stood. "Have you heard about the execution?"

I nodded. "What are people saying about it?"

"They're excited. Such a thing has never happened. Everyone's going," Jo explained.

"Huh." The excitement part had thrown me into a state of sorrow once again. "They just don't understand what's really happening."

"What do you mean?" she asked.

"Nothing. Never mind." I forced a smile at her. "I'll be leaving right after that."

"Goodbye, human Anna James."

I chuckled. "Goodbye, Scavegirl Jo. I'll never forget everything you've done for me."

She smiled. "Nor I you."

Ben came to see me later in the morning. "Have you eaten today?" he asked.

"Yes." I looked at him curiously. "Ben?"

He raised his eyebrows as he opened the curtains wider to let more light in. The day seemed unusually dreary outside.

"Is Atavia still saying I have to be in here?" I really wanted to sneak out and talk to Cassie. I had been scheming since Jo left how I was going to get that chance.

"Yes," he answered.

I sighed. "Of course she is."

"She's not going to change her mind, Ms. James," he told me. "She feels more secure with you… secured."

I rolled my eyes. I was so sick of this bed, this room, their queen. "For my lunchtime meal, can I request that the one maidservant who doesn't speak bring me my food?"

He glanced at me, as if trying to read my mind to decide if I were up to something.

"Because," I said quickly. "I don't feel like talking to anyone today. Sometimes the maidservants talk to me. I'm just not in the mood for chitchat, and I know for sure that one won't strike up a conversation."

"I can tell the maidservants not to speak to you," he reassured me.

"No, just send that one. She'll be in and out. And that goes for you, too," I added. "You don't have to check up on me again today. I don't want to be disturbed."

He eyed me up again as I collapsed back onto the bed with my arm over my eyes, as if pouting. I was trying my best to show him a classic human trait and hoped he'd send Cassie. I promised I'd take her back with me. I had to speak with her.

When there was a knock on my door around noon, I jumped out of bed realizing I had fallen asleep with my arm still covering my eyes. It took me a moment to realize where I was, as if I had dreamt this entire thing.

I licked my dry lips and walked over to the door, praying it was Cassie. "Come in," I shouted.

The door opened and in she came, the only other human on Evadere. I saw Ben standing right outside the door. I briefly glanced at him and then shut the door behind Cassie.

"They said you requested me," Cassie hissed. "What's going on?"

"We don't have much time to talk," I whispered back, looking around is if there were cameras on me. "I needed to tell you I'm leaving."

"Where? To Earth?" she asked.

"Yes," I answered. "Right after Mrs. Anderson's execution."

"The witch?" she asked.

"Yeah, that's her," I whispered. "I'm meeting up with Emry right after, and then he's transporting me back. Are you coming with me?"

She hesitated and looked at her hands, realizing she still held the tray. She set it down on a small table.

"You don't want to go now?" I asked. I couldn't believe she was even considering staying here with Atavia.

"I'm just worried that the Queen will somehow find out I've deceived her all these years," Cassie confessed.

I glanced back at the door, realizing every extra moment with Cassie would be suspicious to Ben.

"She won't. Just find me during the execution and stay close by. Your family misses you."

"Another thing I'm worried about is going back. I've always dreamt of it, but actually doing it..."

"You've got to go now. Ben will be wondering why you're still in here," I told her. "You're a human, Cassie. You didn't ask to be here. It's time you got your chance to go back home."

Chapter 14

I watched out the window the following day. Groups of contributors poured into the castle yard, crowding together. They were all dressed nicely in gowns and white suits, while Atavia's servants kept trying to keep them all happy with replenished tables of food and drink.

Ben knocked and entered my room. He came up behind me and stood with his hands folded behind his back.

"What are all these contributors doing here?" I questioned him.

He looked out the window from over my shoulder. "Today's the day."

"Execution day?"

He nodded. "I guess you're in the mood to talk today?"

I frowned at his sarcasm. "Yeah."

"You've changed your mood again," he pointed out.

"I didn't know it was going to be today. Today is when I go back to Earth, then," I stated.

He walked over to the bookshelf, and then turned around to face me. "I thought you didn't want to be here?"

"I just want to be with Emry."

"The future king has responsibilities here. I'm not a relationship counselor. I don't know how to help fix your emotions."

Ben always seemed so calm, like a machine. "I'm not asking you to fix anything. Never mind.

You're a contributor. You don't get it. And aren't you the least bit sad yourself?"

"Why should I be?" he asked.

"Because it's your sister who is being publicly executed today."

"I figured you were going to refer to that." He sighed. "Ms. James, my *sister* hasn't been my sister in a very long time, since we were children. She practices a dark magic I've never had the intention of getting involved with. Just because we share the same blood line... she's ill, as I see it. She's done nothing but center her life on attempting to destroy the royal blood line. She's had second and third chances, and it's always turned out the same. It's time we've rid ourselves of her."

Amazing that he could just wash his hands of her so easily. He showed no remorse, no feeling. How I wished I could be like that today. I just wanted to be numb of all of the feelings I had of Emry Logan and rid myself of them once and for all.

"So all these contributors have come to witness this horrific thing that's about to happen?" I asked.

He nodded. "Queen Atavia has invited all contributors. She needs to patch up her reputation after what's happened to Raleigh, and she needs to set an example."

"These people see it as a party?"

"Most of these people are just excited to set foot within the bounds of the castle as they've never had the opportunity before."

"And you don't think the Scaves will come?" I pried.

He pressed his lips together into a tight smile. "We're on high alert security-wise, Ms. James. It's all under control. If there's nothing else you need, I have my duties to tend to."

I shook my head.

"Someone will be up to get you later this evening."

"Anna James?"

The door opened. I straightened out my long blue gown with my hands and nervously glanced up at the servant who had come to take me out to the castle yard.

"Ready?" she asked.

"Yeah." I looked in a mirror in the corner of the room. My hair was pulled back in a similar fashion as I had seen all the contributors wearing theirs today. I had found dark pink lipstick and smeared it onto my cheeks and lips. I wanted to look stunning for Emry. I took a deep breath and left the prison that had been my room.

Once in the hallway, there were contributors everywhere, chatting and holding up glasses of alcohol. They had been here most of the day, and

I assumed they were drunk, laughing giddily and chatting amongst themselves. A couple of them looked my way as I walked past, but they didn't know who I was. I was just another contributor to them.

My heels clanked against the hard, cement stairs as I followed the servant, who kept glancing back at me as if I were going to run away. I could only imagine how tired all of Atavia's staff must be from tending to all of these people since this morning.

Once outside, I inhaled the sweet, fresh air. I could barely move as everyone stood shoulder to shoulder.

"Okay," the servant said. "I'm supposed to tell you that you're being watched, so don't try anything funny."

I raised my eyebrows. "Okay... thanks for letting me know." I turned away from her and pushed my way through the people toward the front. I couldn't see a thing.

"Hey, watch it!" a man shouted out as I bumped into him and his overflowing glass of wine spilled all over his shoes.

I ignored him and kept moving through the mass. There were guards perched upon balconies of the castle, weapons in hand, as they overlooked the people and beyond in case any Scaves were to make an attempt to attack. Perhaps they were there for me, too, I thought. Up ahead was a large podium made out of fresh wood as it obviously had recently been built just for this *occasion*.

"Ms. James, I see you've made it."

I glared up into the smug face of Treyu. He slurped another sip of his drink and licked his top lip as he grinned at me.

"And front row, too. Very impressive to see you in touch with your dark side." Treyu threw back his head and laughed uncontrollably at himself.

I glared, furious at just the mere sight of him. He stumbled away, grabbing the hand of a woman next to him and kissing it. I was grateful for her distraction so that he was away from me.

Music played in the distance, the base booming over the voices of the contributors. Everywhere I looked people were dancing and eating, laughing and drinking. This really was a party to them. I wondered if anyone had a clue as to what was going to happen. I wondered if death was so nonchalant to everyone on Evadere. To everyone here it seemed as if death was just the means to an end. They could "rid" themselves of someone that way. To me, it was an uncertainty, a permanent stripping of one's spirit, and if that spirit was taken away by this sort of cruelty, it made it that much worse. Evadere had no court system. Queen Atavia made all the decisions, and she based those on her hatred. I was ashamed to be part of this, but I had to be here to find Emry, to get out of Evadere, and to take Cassie Banesberry with me.

Someone screamed as two guards walked up onto the podium holding Mrs. Anderson, who cried out and carried on. The guards could barely restrain her and had to keep grabbing her thrashing arms and legs as she kicked and threw her body in all directions.

There was a short, wide pole in the center of the podium, more like a stage at this point, as the crowd cheered louder and louder with each move of desperation Mrs. Anderson made to get away.

After multiple attempts, the guards were finally able to bound her against the pole, her hands tied behind her and her feet wrapped together as she continued to lash about, now whimpering as the ropes cut into her frail skin. Some of the contributors were screaming obscenities at her. Then she just stood there, realizing she was unable to escape. I wondered what was going through her mind at that moment as she made acceptance with her fate.

Suddenly, Mrs. Anderson locked eyes with mine, her face wild and full of despair. She scowled at me, and I turned away. She had always been so strange to me, even on Earth. She had this dark way about her, yet had been so calm before. Seeing her so on edge was even more disturbing. I thought about how she had made attacks on Emry and wanted him locked up in prison on Earth. She had blamed me then for getting in the way of her plans. I'm sure her scowling at me was just another way of saying she blamed me now for what was about to happen to her.

The music stopped and the contributors seemed to all quiet their voices at the same time. Mrs. Anderson stood up on her stage all alone facing the crowd. Just below the podium, royalty lined up one by one. Treyu saw his family and stumbled as he rushed to get over to where they were. Atavia was in the middle, Emry by her side. He looked so handsome in his white suit outlined in gold trim. He had a small crown on his head that he lifted proudly.

Out of the corner of my eye I saw a little wave. Looking over, I saw Cassie appearing from behind a robust contributor woman. I nodded to her so she knew I saw her, and then she disappeared again as the contributor stepped in front, blocking my view.

"Welcome, my dear friends," Atavia said.

The crowd cheered.

Atavia beamed at their response. "Today we rid our planet of one more evil."

They held up their glasses and toasted to Mrs. Anderson's demise.

"And this, dear friends, is your future king, my son, Emry." She gestured toward him and clapped her hands. Emry grinned and waved to his people, who grew even louder with shouting and clapping.

He turned around and looked at Mrs. Anderson. "Do you have anything you'd like to say?" he asked her.

Mrs. Anderson tried again and again to break away from the ropes that held her in place. She gritted her teeth and thrashed her head about.

Atavia looked absolutely delighted in her reaction. "Anything she'd have to say would be mere nonsense, anyway." She chuckled. She glanced up at her guards still watching over the boundaries of the castle yard. She then searched through the crowd, her eyes resting upon my face. She gave me a satisfied look as if saying good riddance to me also, knowing I'd soon be gone and back to Earth.

I waited for the executioner to get up on the podium. I wondered if Mrs. Anderson was going to be beheaded, hung, or shot, but nothing was happening. Then all of the royalty joined hands.

"This is bigger than you all!" Mrs. Anderson cried out. "They're going to control all of you!

Murderers! Murderers!"

Atavia looked at the rest of the royal family. They all laughed and mocked Mrs. Anderson. "I told you, nonsense," Atavia said, smiling.

They resumed holding hands and lining up. Their backs were toward the podium. Mrs. Anderson was still screaming out, trying to get someone to listen to her. I looked around for Ben. He was nowhere in sight. I looked over at Cassie again, who was staring at Mrs. Anderson with her mouth open. At least one person here didn't find joy in such a public display of disgust.

I watched Emry close his eyes, along with the rest of his family. They began concentrating. Almost instantly as soon as their eyes closed, Mrs. Anderson began shrieking. This time it wasn't screaming from being bound to the pole, it was one of extreme physical pain.

I stared at Emry, at Atavia's face. I went down the row of royalty, seven in all. They stood strong, joined together. They were using their powers to kill her. Mrs. Anderson's body twisted and trembled as she continued to cry out, as if she were being burned alive. I felt a burning in the pit of my stomach.

"Emry, stop this!" I yelled out, but I doubted if even the contributor beside me had heard. The crowd cheered and screamed as Mrs. Anderson's pain increased. Her cries were so shrill, they rose higher above the crowd. Some of the contributors laughed. Others looked outraged that she wasn't dead yet.

"Die, witch, die!" they chanted.

The burning in my stomach increased. I felt a pain radiate from my toes up my legs. My knees buckled. I fell to the ground. The burning in my stomach reached my lungs. I struggled to breathe. Then an intense throbbing entered my head. My eyes felt as if they were bulging and about to burst. I reached in the air for help. One of the contributors beside me stepped on my other hand that had been on the ground. I forced my head up to look at Mrs. Anderson. She was convulsing now, her head rattling back and forth as if it could roll right off her neck. She was still shrieking. I looked at the royal line again. Everyone's eyes remained closed, except one. Atavia. She was staring directly at me. My skin prickled, as if on fire.

Atavia's using her powers on me. She's going to kill me. No one even knows what's going on.

Her eyes were fierce and full of disgust. She loathed every inch of me. This was perfect. Emry was distracted. Everyone was distracted. No one would even notice what was happening to me until it was too late.

My body curled into a ball on the ground. I felt the tremors come on. Every inch of me felt like it was blazing. My eyeballs continued to swell. I knew I had to do something.

Scream, you idiot. Scream like Mrs. Anderson.

So I did. I let the pain escape from my throat. It hurt so bad. I wasn't going to be able to take much more. I cried out a long, shrill screech. Still, over my own cries, I could hear Mrs. Anderson. Her pain was even greater than mine. She had everyone else using their powers against her. I only had Atavia, and still it was unbearable.

Now my insides felt as if they were melting together, like I could dissolve into a puddle on this cursed ground and evaporate into nothing.

I felt someone's hands on my face. They seemed very hot. "Anna! Anna!" someone cried out.

I struggled to open my heavy eyes. I wasn't even sure I'd be able to see. My arms contracted in at my sides. I could barely make out a face. It was Cassie.

"What's going on?" Cassie covered her mouth in horror as if she was figuring it all out. She stood up and stared at Atavia. "Stop!" she yelled. "Emry, stop it! She's killing her! Atavia's killing Anna!"

My head turned toward the podium. Mrs. Anderson hung limp, still tied to the pole. Royalty still held hands. Cassie now ran full throttle toward them. The guards blocked her.

"No!" she screamed. "Anna's dying! Let me through to Emry! Emry, please!"

The crowd quieted down.

Emry squinted his eyes to see Cassie and what she was pointing at, which was me still in a ball in severe pain. My muscles contracted harder. He tried to let go of his mother's hand, but she wouldn't let go of him. Her face twisted up in pure hatred as she intended to finish what she started.

"Stop!" Emry yelled at her.

Royalty looked around at each other, everyone in confusion about what was going on.

"I said, stop!" Emry had that look on his face. It was one of both despair and anger as he realized that everything I had assumed about his mother had been true, and now she was destroying me, getting rid of me so I'd be out of her precious son's life forever.

Everything went blurry. I heard someone else cry out. It sounded like Atavia. Then all of a sudden the pain stopped. I felt full amounts of air enter my lungs as my chest heaved and lapped the oxygen around me. I was alive. My muscles that had been contracting were now humming with a dull ache from the violent movements they had been forced into. I opened my watery eyes. Someone wrapped their arms around me and picked me up off the ground. It was Emry. He looked down at me. Now fatigue took the place of the pain. I tried to open my lips to say something. He pressed his finger to my mouth so I wouldn't try to speak. His eyes were full of compassion and relief.

"You were so right, Anna. You're always right. Why couldn't I have just trusted you from the beginning? She was out to get you, both of us," he whispered.

Then a loud cackling laugh was heard from the direction of the podium. I made a poor attempt to move my head to see who it was coming from. Mrs. Anderson? No, she was still lifeless at the pole.

Atavia threw back her head in a smug manner and laughed again.

"Oh, my dear, dear son, you have so much to learn yet." She took a few steps closer to us. "You actually tried to use your powers on *me*?" Then she chuckled again. "Your powers are mundane compared to what I can do."

Emry huffed at his mother as he huddled me closer, as if he could protect me by being my shield.

"Leave her alone, Mother. I love her."

"You can't love a human," she said mockingly. "Being raised on Earth has made you soft. Let her go. You'll find someone else suitable here."

"Stay away from us," he warned.

"Or what? You'll use your powers on me again?" She laughed hysterically. "I barely felt your weak attempt."

The queen inched her way closer and closer to where Emry stood clinging onto me. My mouth felt arid. A headache was forming from whatever it was that had happened to me moments ago.

"You see, Emry, I don't need to cling onto your power in order to carry out my intentions. I can kill that pathetic human while you're holding onto her. Better say your goodbyes, my son. This is for your own good." Atavia took one more step toward us.

Emry looked around in desperation for somewhere to run. There were contributors everywhere as they witnessed yet another show, only this one more shocking to them as their cheers were now silenced. It would be too difficult to outrun his mother's powers. He looked at me, his expression pained.

"I'm so, so sorry," he said, tears streaming down his cheeks. "I know now that there's only two things that I want."

"What's that?" I whispered, my voice raspy and low.

"Either where you go, I go, or where I go, you go." He made a sad attempt to give me a smile.

"Oh, so pathetic," Atavia hissed, rolling her eyes. "A human with my son, the king? Completely out of the question."

"This *human* is going to be my wife," Emry told her. "She is going to be queen." Atavia's eyes grew large at his words. Her mouth dropped open.

I felt my heart throb within me. He had just said he was going to marry me. He had told his mother that.

"You say your goodbyes, Mother, to me. I'm leaving this place. I'm transporting Anna back to Earth." Emry gave her a stern look.

Atavia attempted to gain her composure from his previous statement of queen and me being connected together. "It will only take a moment for me to finish killing your human." She focused her eyes on me again and grew very still. Her body stiffened.

I closed my eyes, waiting for the pain to return, praying that instead I'd open them back up to

Seneca, Ohio, back to the normalcy of Earth and its selfish human race where supernatural powers were merely a myth.

"What?" Atavia screamed out.

My eyes snapped open. Emry was still holding me. Atavia just stood there in disbelief.

"It can't be!" the queen cried. She glared at her son.

"What's happening?" I whispered.

Emry smirked. "It worked."

"What did?" I asked.

"I used my powers on her."

Atavia's body stiffened once more as she tried again to use her powers on me. Nothing happened.

"I used my powers to take away yours," Emry explained to her.

Atavia's face went pale. She clutched herself, as if naked. "What? This is ... impossible." Emry's smile widened. "You're now powerless," Emry told her.

"The queen's powerless?" a contributor shouted out in alarm. "You mean, she's now a Scave?"

Emry looked at me and nudged my nose with his nose. Then he looked back to Atavia. "That's right, Mother. Queen Atavia, the Scave."

Atavia gasped.

Epilogue

A slight breeze tousled my hair as I stepped out of the car and stared up at the big, abandoned house. Cassie stood in the overgrown yard, her arms crossed in front of her. Emry walked up behind me and placed his hand on my back.

"Well, we did it," I whispered. "Back home to Seneca as promised."

Cassie frowned. Her eyes shifted to a broken window at the edge of the porch. "This isn't how I remember it at all."

My heart broke for poor Cassie. She didn't have much to return to, but at least she had been fortunate enough to return. She was no longer under the dominion of Atavia and could make a new start on Earth, where she belonged.

My thoughts wandered to Atavia, Evadere's now powerless queen. I could picture her scowling in the depths of the dungeon as the castle she once controlled now held her prisoner. The contributors had turned on her once they had learned she had been stripped of all power. They probably would've killed her if not for Emry, who was able to calm the crowd. They chanted out, "King Emry!" as the guards carried Atavia off to the dungeon.

"I'm ready to go see my mother," Cassie said, her eyes full of sadness as she turned away from the house.

"Right through this little patch of woods." I motioned for her and Emry to follow as I led the way, remembering how I had followed Lucy, Cassie's cousin's little girl when I had been trying to dig up information about Mrs. Anderson's past. I knew that Cassie's mother had aged and was debilitated both mentally and physically as I remembered her wheelchair bound and asleep. More than likely, she'd no longer be able to recognize her beloved missing daughter after all these years. I didn't know how to prep Cassie for it, or how to comfort her as she realized that time changes everything, and everyone.

Together, we walked to the front door of where Cassie's mother lived. A soft glow came from one of the windows.

"Ready?" I asked her.

Cassie turned around to face me. She held both of my hands in her own. "Anna, thank you, for everything. Emry, you, too." She smiled at him. "I wish the both of you luck in your life together." She turned and looked at the door again. "This is something I need to do by myself."

"There's going to be a lot of questions. Are you sure you don't want us there for support?" Emry asked.

She pressed her lips together. "No, really. I'm fine."

Emry took my hand as I waved one last time to Cassie before heading back to the path through the woods.

"Don't worry about her," Emry said. "She's tough. She survived all that time with my mother, didn't she?"

I nodded as I looked up into his eyes. "So, now what?"

Emry stopped walking and grinned. "Well, I was thinking..."

I raised my eyebrows. "Uh oh..."

He chuckled. "What do you say we go back to Evadere and work on making you queen?"

Queen Anna. I liked the way it sounded. "And the contributors and Scaves?"

"We have a lot of work to do, don't we?"

"That's an understatement," I said.

"Do you still want to be queen, *my* queen?" He sounded a little nervous about how I felt.

"Wherever you go, I go."

He grinned and held out his hands. I placed mine in his and closed my eyes, knowing that when I opened them again, we'd be back in Evadere.

Acknowledgements

I am so grateful for the support of all of my family and friends who have encouraged me to hurry up and finish another book, especially to my dad, Dennis James Payne, always checking in to see my progress and when I'll be finished with another one, and of course to my husband, Brad Zook, who continues to support my writing every day.

Also, to those who are reading my work and encouraging me to keep going, thank you so very much!

Good reviews are important to a novel's success. If you enjoyed Evadere, please be kind and leave a review wherever you purchased the book.

Sincerely,

Sara V. Zook

About the Author:

Sara V. Zook graduated from the University of Pittsburgh at Johnstown in 2004 with a creative writing degree. She works full-time from home and also takes care of her young children. Loving to read romance novels with a fantasy twist, she decided to write one of her own.

She was born and raised in Pennsylvania where she resides still with her husband, Brad, and their three children, Coen, Avery and Lucas.

Contact Sara V. Zook

Website: http://www.saravzook.com

Email: svzook@gmail.com

www.ingramcontent.com/pod-product-compliance
Lightning Source LLC
Chambersburg PA
CBHW061303170626
46817CB00001B/25